I0682514

A Sinister Spring in Edgemont

Village of Edgemont, Volume 3

Della North

Published by Lynda French, 2023.

A SINISTER SPRING IN EDGEMONT

First edition. September 30, 2023.

ISBN: 978-1998074082

Written by Della North.

A heartfelt thank you to Darlene Hartung for her wonderful encouragement, it means a lot.

Chapter One

Tuesday, April 21, 2020

My life has changed and become so much better this past year, muses Barbie Nichols, getting out of the tub to apply moisturizing lotion. Her reminiscing occurs, as it usually does, while she's admiring her roomy, luxurious bathroom. They've only been in this house for a month and everything about it is still new and delightful to her. Winding down before bedtime she continues thinking back, and feeling grateful for this grand life.

On this day last year Greg injured his wrist at work and I was so worried about losing his income. I only made minimum wage hairdressing and we were already dodging calls from bill collectors. Then two weeks later I won the lottery. Well, I didn't win it all, but a 3-way split on $52 million worked out to be more than 17 million dollars. 17 MILLION DOLLARS! What a windfall, I still can't believe it.

According to the news this Covid-19 pandemic is changing the whole world, but the lottery money is protecting me from that too. It doesn't matter that the salon and the trucking company and the school all had to close, we're financially secure. Barbie savours that phrase, repeating it a couple of times, before settling into bed enjoying her thankfulness and wearing a satisfied smile.

John Seely likes living in Edgemont Village but feels Margaret, his daughter, will have a better chance if they move far away from the area. Edgemont is too small since the family's dirty laundry has become common knowledge. *And it's quite a bit more than just dirty laundry,* he reminds himself.

Properties here never stay on the market for long but even so he is surprised and pleased at how quickly he is able to conclude the sale. A cash offer makes all the difference: no conditions and no financing. The new owner is a local hairdresser who won the lottery.

Barbie Nichols never dreamed that someday she'd live in Edgemont's Executive Estates. Her goal has been moving up from renting the main floor of a bungalow to a mobile home in the Edgemont Trailer Park. Even that dream seemed impossibly out of reach. The lottery win makes such a difference. Everyone knows a win will change their lives but until it happens it's beyond imagination.

Too bad it's caused so much trouble in the family.

News about a lottery winner's tragic end is always featured as a top story. Whether it's because the public suffers from envy or *schadenfreude* the item gets plenty of attention, focusing on the downside of winning. The news anchors seem to gloat over rags-to-riches-to-rags tales, suicides, divorces, and even murders.

For most people winning the lottery is good luck, but although Barbie Nichols herself enjoyed every minute of her new-found wealth it turned out to be a curse. At least she died quickly enough not to have any regrets.

Covid-19 Update: An announcement is made that for the first time in its history there will be no Calgary Stampede rodeo and fair in 2020. Not even two World Wars shut down the famous parade. To date Covid-19 has claimed the lives of 68 Albertans and the province is in a state of emergency.

Chapter Two

Wednesday, April 22, 2020

Grant has come over to Judith's apartment but not for long, he's waiting on the call to handle the investigation into Barbie Nichols' death. Meanwhile she's made coffee and they're drinking it while nibbling on cookies.

"Who, and how, is your new partner?" Judith asks and Grant tells her all he knows about the man, and also gives her his impressions.

Detective First Class Reginald *call me Reg* Osborne, a recent transfer in from the Maritimes, is close to retirement. His age is the only concern Grant feels about his new partner.

Reg is a knowledgeable, even-tempered, affable man. He doesn't smoke, vape, or chew tobacco, and if he drinks there is never a whiff of alcohol sweating out of his system. His wardrobe is unexciting, but he always appears neat and professional-looking. His social life seems to revolve around family get-togethers with his four adult children and their families. He is divorced, and a widower, and a grandfather.

He isn't much of a talker, and doesn't volunteer personal information, but answers fully when asked. Grant and Reg have been partnered for three weeks now and are getting along fine. Reg is comfortable to be around, and he's a steady, easy-going driver which suits Grant who often gets impatient behind the wheel.

Reg explains that he's been learning his way around Edgemont and the surrounding villages adding:

"I like driving, I find it relaxing. And I'm starting to get my bearings. Someone once told me it takes three months to feel at home in a new place but I can tell already that I'm going to like living here."

Grant hasn't discussed retirement with Reg and he tries to sound the man out to get an idea about his plans.

"I've never been to any of the Atlantic provinces but I heard it's beautiful there, a popular destination for tourists and retirees."

"It is, especially tourism. I have no idea how folks will manage now they've closed the provinces down because of this virus."

"Oh right, I heard something about that. Actually, it was an article about someone in the middle of moving house being told they couldn't go into New Brunswick from Nova Scotia, or vice versa? I can't remember the details."

"It's crazy, that whole area is too interconnected to have closed borders."

"I guess the Premiers will just have to work it out – or maybe the Federal Government will get involved? The Maritimes has always been a Liberal stronghold so..."

"That's true. I make it a rule to never discuss politics at work or socially."

Grant took the hint and changed direction: "Whereabouts did you live?"

"Amherst. Pretty as a picture in summer and popular with artists and craftspeople. Lots of market-garden type farming in the community, and of course, great seafood. It's great having the ocean nearby although I find the Atlantic to be cold all year round. I really do not like the winters in Nova Scotia."

Grant huffs a laugh and asks: "Do you really thing the weather will be better in Alberta?"

"I do! Go ahead and laugh, but you'd know what I mean if you ever felt the bone-chilling damp that comes off the water in winter. And even though it doesn't get very cold, I mean -20 is generally the worst, we get huge, really huge, dumps of snow all at once."

"Winters here haven't seemed as cold as when I was a kid, but maybe everybody thinks that? however we usually stay in the high minus-twenties with a couple of weeks of -35 or so every year. February is our coldest month, March is our snowiest, and we have green Christmases fairly often, maybe that's climate change?"

"Minus mid-thirties sure does sound cold but they say it's a dry cold and that makes a difference."

"Yeah, expect to have badly chapped lips your first winter here. But on most days we have beautiful blue skies with tons of sunshine. Our weather always seems to be better than Edmonton's, probably because we're so close to the Rockies."

"Once I get settled in here I plan to do plenty of exploring in the mountains and all these Provincial Parks. I plan to end my days living as an Albertan, but not for some time yet!" Reg chuckles.

After Grant relates that conversation he'd had with Reg Judith comments: "He sounds like a nice man. I never thought Suzanne was a nice woman so I hope you and Reg will work well together."

"I think we will. He's got many years of experience but there's much more to it than *time served*. There's the intelligence necessary to process all the insights picked up along the way. One good thing, though, is that despite his age he doesn't discriminate."

"Oh, now you're discriminating, Grant. I believe that's called ageism–"

Judith doesn't get to finish her gibe before Grant half-wrestles her into a hug saying:

"You know what I mean. Lots of the older cops tell racist and sexist jokes or make assumptions that perpetuate systemic discrimination within the police force."

"Like profiling?"

"No, profiling is different, it's based on facts and statistics. Like insurance companies use when they charge young male drivers higher rates than females."

"Um, just because the insurance companies do the same thing doesn't make it right. Their self-interest is evident and they're all about the bottom line."

"And that's why profiling is only one tool in the policeman's tool-box, and it's fluid because the stats from six or seven years ago no longer apply. Don't get me started on the fairness of that argument, it's based on sound logic and it is flexible when it should be."

Sitting back up straight on the couch and finger-combing her hair back in place Judith announces:

"We'll shelve that discussion for now, then. So what's happening with Barbie Nichols?"

"What have people been saying? and did you know her? What can you tell me about her?"

"Her three daughters attend our school, they were subsidized but now well, now Barbie is the one offering financial help with her lottery winnings which is so nice. Well, it was. There is a fourth daughter,

Brenda's twin, but there's something wrong, behavioural problems I think, and she's home-schooled.

There's also a son of Greg Nichols' from his first marriage, so he's Barbie's stepson, but I don't know anything about it except that he's older than the girls."

"Well, yeah," Grant says with a smile.

"Oh! I see what you mean. No, the twins are from Barbie's first... well, not a marriage and I'm not even sure if they were together long enough to qualify as common-law? Hmm, anyhow he's not in the picture. He's dead."

"So both Barbie and Greg Nichols brought children into their marriage and then had two daughters themselves?"

"Yes, that's right. Brenda is in her final year with us so she must be about seventeen. I believe her half-sisters are eight and eleven."

"You get a lot of mixed or I guess the right word is *extended* families nowadays, don't you?"

"We do, and It's fine. Our only concern is that no one has access to the girls in our school unless they're on an approved list. The onus is on the legal guardian to keep us updated but we still send out reminders a few times a year. People change romantic partners quite a bit, Grant."

His smile turns into a grin as pulls her close for a kiss.

"You just keep getting dragged into the big, bad, old world, eh?" he teases fondly.

Judith's upbringing was sheltered to protect the secret of her mother's alcoholism. She never had any close friends until recently, and Grant is her first boyfriend. She thinks the words boyfriend and girlfriend are silly at their age but there's no way she'll refer to him as her lover! Meeting his gaze with these thoughts in her head makes her blush. Grant's eyes sparkle at her but he says:

"Never mind distracting me, woman. I'm on call and I'll have to leave quickly."

Judith just shakes her head but she can't stop smiling. Bringing herself back to the topic at hand she explains:

"You know, some of the parents get quite huffy if we use the wrong names. I've found that most of the mothers keep the same surname as their children, at least in their dealings with the school, but not everyone. In fact, Barbie Nichols' oldest, Brenda, is called Nikovics and her two youngest are called Nichols."

"I'm just going to make a note of that," says Grant, typing into his phone. "Can you spell it for me?"

Judith does so explaining that Nikovics was Barbie Nichols' maiden name. She has no idea was the father of the girls is, or was, called.

"Same initials, that's convenient."

"I don't imagine the Nikovics ever had much, if any, engraved or monogrammed belongings. Still you're right when it comes to initialing stuff."

"So the family is what.. Eastern European?"

"Just Barbie's father. Her mother's an Irishwoman, Moira, and I've met her a few times recently. She's raised her granddaughters and they've now all moved here to live together with Barbie and her second family."

"That's very odd, isn't it?"

"Oh I forgot to mention! The father of Barbie's twins was an abuser. Shortly after the twins were born she dumped them on her mother and disappeared. He became violent with Moira and she had him arrested. He went to jail for awhile but when he came out he did the exact same thing again except he managed to escape custody and disappeared into the Kananaskis backcountry. He was pursued and there was a manhunt. It was on the news."

"I remember some of that. The hunt for him turned into a search-and-rescue and then a body retrieval because he was presumed to have drowned. He had a European name as well, but I don't recall it. I'll have to get someone to dig up the file for me. They never did find his body, right?"

"Oh, I don't know. But that would explain... hmm, that would explain why Moira Nikovics kept the girls instead of returning them to Barbie when she resurfaced."

"Where was she?"

"Apparently working cash jobs in the National Parks. Travelling from Banff to Lake Louise to Yoho, waitressing or housekeeping, stuff like that. She's a qualified hairdresser too. That's the work she was doing when her younger girls got enrolled in the school."

"And the family qualified for your subsidy?"

"Yes, because Greg Nichols works in a warehouse and drives a local delivery truck so he doesn't have a big paycheque, and Barbie just made minimum wage hairdressing. She worked with Dana Lezinsky, do you remember her?"

"Holly's mother, of course. I wonder if I'll be interviewing her again this time."

"What exactly is *this time* all about, Grant?" All I heard is that Barbie Nichols is dead and she was killed while asleep in her own bed."

"I don't know a lot more except that it's definitely murder. She was smothered with a pillow and died of asphyxiation. The pillow was still over her face, no effort made to hide it."

"Suffocated while she slept! That's horrible. She would have fought back, right?"

"There's a lot we don't know. If someone was pressing down with both hands and their body weight it would take about four minutes to fatally cut off the air supply. If Barbie Nichols was deeply asleep when the attack began she might not have struggled that much, and if she'd taken a sleeping pill or had a couple of drinks before bed, well... That information will all come to light after the autopsy."

The graphic description of Barbie's death had brought tears to Judith's eyes. Grant pulled her into a tight embrace and apologized.

"No, no Grant. You can always tell me, in fact I want you to. I want you to know that you can confide in me, or use me as a sounding-board. I'm only crying because Barbie was such a nice woman. She really was. Always joking – even when she was complaining about something she'd still make you laugh. And she laughed a lot, too. Her life was difficult and I remember when I heard about her lottery win my first thought was *it couldn't have happened to a more deserving person.*"

Judith cries a little more before moving out of the comfort of Grant's arms. Wiping her eyes she asks if he wants another coffee or maybe a bite to eat?

"No, thanks hon. Those shortbread cookies were delicious. I can't believe I ate so many, did you bake them?"

"Don't be silly," Judith laughs. "Why would I bake when I can buy real Walkers Shortbread, imported straight from Scotland? I doubt if I could make them for what Costco charges. Do you know how much a pound of butter costs? and a batch of shortbread must take at least one pound."

"I'm joking!" he laughs. "I saw you open the package, remember?"

The sad moment has passed just as Grant's phone rings and he has to leave. Before he heads out Judith pulls him back to the kitchen where she's now placed a bar of soap by the sink, reminding him:

"Don't forget the new rule about disinfecting your hands when entering and leaving any place."

Brian really rocks the casual look of faded jeans and sweatshirt, thinks Lila looking up at the tall man walking beside her. They were on a short hike, one of the few activities still allowed these days.

Brian Penner has dark red hair, blue eyes, and the strong physique of a construction worker. She's very aware of his presence, especially since he's hovering over her in a protective manner. A recent widow, Lila is feeling fragile yet she's enjoying Brian's companionship and is having trouble reconciling those feelings.

She'd fallen out of love with her husband but would have stayed in her marriage if he'd behaved differently. The manner of his death destroyed any residual feeling she had left, but there are other losses and she was just learning how to cope with that.

Brian's wife had died ten years ago of cancer. His teenage daughter, Beth, had been encouraging him to find someone for awhile now but it wasn't until he met Lila Morelli that his interest was piqued.

Lila, with her bubbly good nature and gurgling laugh. Her pretty face and petite figure. Typical of Lila's personality that she adds streaks of pink or purple or blue to her lovely blonde curls the way other women will paint their fingernails to match their outfit. It's no surprise that Lila has caught Brian Penner's eye, she's the kind of person people notice – both men and women.

"Lila honey I know it's way, way too soon for me to say anything to you, but I just want to be sure that you understand I'm here ready and waiting for whenever you're ready. I hope that won't take too long, but whatever time you need is yours. I'm not going anywhere."

Lila was enjoying the low rumble of Brian's deep voice before registering his words and when she did realize what he was saying she drew in her breath with a gasp. He immediately put his arm around her shoulders but held it there lightly, gentling and soothing her.

"I'm sorry if I seem pushy, Lila. I just wanted to be sure you knew how I felt. But you do know, right? You knew before you even went back to Toronto, didn't you?"

"I suspected as much, Brian and I'm flattered, truly, but–"

He touches his finger to her lips signalling her to hush, she doesn't need to say anything now. The look of concern leaves her face and is replaced by a sweet smile. It takes all of Brian's restraint to hold back from kissing those lovely lips.

"We'd better hurry and catch Beth up before we lose sight of her."

"Well we certainly won't lose her in the crowd!" quips Brian.

Covid-19 Update: Rules and regulations are being discussed and recommended by Federal, Provincial, and City governments and Health Authorities. There's so much uncertainty, and *two weeks to flatten the curve* is now at five weeks and counting.

Chapter Three

Wednesday, April 22, 2020

"What the hell, Gary? what are you doing in my purse?" demands Brenda finding her stepbrother digging into her bag. She turns to Glenda saying: "You better check your money too, Gee, Gary might have stolen it."

The sisters have come into Brenda's room only to find their stepbrother, older by just a few years, already there.

"Hey, it's important. I gotta get out of here. The police will think I killed your Mom."

"Did you?"

"What? no way! what's the matter with you?"

"Then why are you running?"

"Duh, I'm the stepson who has no job, always broke... of course they're going to suspect me."

"They're going to suspect us all and I had thirty bucks in my wallet Gary, so give it back," says Glenda with her hand stuck out.

"Shit, no, I need it. I've really gotta go."

"Gary...:"

"Okay listen, your Mom and I had a big fight. Another one. She and my Dad fought about something and when he took off she was still pissed and took it out on me."

"About what?"

"The same stuff, as usual, I have to get a job or go to school, either/or, otherwise I have to find someplace else to live. I mean, how the fu, uh, hell am I going to do that with no money? So I asked if she'd stake me some funds upfront, just to get me settled like, and she laughed her head off. I mean, seriously, she's rolling in it. Would it kill her to give..."

The three teenagers give each other scared looks.

"Yeah, good one. You're such a loser, Gary. Gimme back my money now."

"No, I told you, I gotta go, they'll be after me."

"Oh you're so dramatic, Gary. You just react without thinking."

"Do not! Listen, how does this sound *oh yeah Officer, I was home at the time but I didn't do anything to Barbie.* They'll take one look at me and won't bother looking at anyone else. I mean I really was here but that's no alibi. I spent almost every minute in my room and didn't see nobody or talk to anybody–"

"I heard you. I heard your horrible music playing, very loudly."

"That doesn't prove anything, though."

"Well, I also heard you thumping about. I don't know why you're always wearing your boots in the house but I heard you going stomp, stomp, stomp as usual."

Smirking, her twin joins the conversation to ask: "Were you dancing, Gary?"

"Just you shut up Glenda," the young man replies with a heavy frown on his red face.

Ignoring him she turns to Brenda asking: "Have you ever seen him dance? He struts around like he thinks he's Mick Jagger. He even does the pursed-up lips thing," and the two of them start laughing.

"Geez, Gary, couldn't you imitate someone from our generation at least?"

"Yeah, instead of like... our grandparents?"

"Aw, to hell with you two," he snarls and, as Brenda had pointed out, stalks off with his uncommonly heavy tread.

"Hey! get back here, loser! You've still got our money."

After the twins successfully recover their cash they return to Brenda's bedroom since it's tidy, to talk out their thoughts.

"I fought with Mom too, you know."

"Oh we're all quarrelling with each other because of being cooped up together so much. Can't even go to the mall."

"No, I mean we fought-fought."

"Are you crazy? with that impaired driving issue hanging over your head you should be acting like the perfect kid until Mom agrees to hire a good lawyer for you."

"No thanks, one perfect kid in this family is enough."

Sighing deeply Brenda asks "What was it about this time?"

"She refuses to use my new name, my name of choice."

"Okay, I'll bite, what's your new name, Gee?"

"Well, it's not Gee anymore. It's Enda, and I want that to be your name too."

"Oh as if... Enda? what kind of a name is that? It's a made-up name and it's stupid."

"Actually it's an Irish name but that's not why I chose it. *Enda* will make it easier for all the lazy pricks around here to not have to say those two consonants distinguishing between you and me. I mean, how much simpler to just say Enda for either of us? We all know that if the voice is complaining, yelling, nagging, or criticizing then it's talking to me, and if the voice is all sweetness and light then it's directed at you."

"Gee, I'm not going to call you Enda and I'm not going to answer if you call me that, either. I sometimes think you're mental."

"Funny, that's what Mom said. Then she told me to shut up, that she chose our names and I'm stuck with mine until I'm eighteen. Then I can change my name legally if I want to. That's what she said. So I said, why Glenda? My father's name wasn't Glen. And she goes, you're a twin and I wanted two names that match. Brenda and Glenda. I was also thinking Tessie and Jessie but those would actually be Theresa and Jessica. This way the name I chose can't be turned into something else by someone else – not even an ungrateful brat."

"So I said that was effing lame and she–"

"No way!"

"I did! but I did say *effing* not, you know."

"And she grounded you, right?"

"No, actually I expected that, but she was already in a bad mood and just told me to go away 'cause she wasn't in the mood for my nonsense."

"Why? I mean, no one's ever in the mood for your crap, but you said she was already in a bad mood so what was that all about?"

"Do you know, I 'm not sure... I mean Mom has been fighting with everybody. Gary, me, Greg, oh and she and Gran had a real blow-out too."

"Not again!"

"Oh and this was something. You know, Gran and Mom can really push each other's buttons... well, they could. Gran was so pissed off, I've never seen her like that. And whatever it was they were fighting about had something to do with us."

"What did you hear?"

"It's what I *didn't* hear... they both shut up as soon as they saw me. Just stopped mid-sentence, mid-argument, just stopped talking – didn't even pretend or try to cover up – just glared at me until I left."

"Yeah, I guess that was kind of obvious. Maybe it was just about you, not us."

"Dream on. They don't see you and I as anything but *us, w*e're just *the twins.* We're lucky we got separate bedrooms. "

"I would have insisted, I mean honestly Gee you're such a slob. Like is there anything actually hanging in any of your closets?"

Glenda pulls open the door of first one of Brenda's closets and then the other. The clothes hang neatly, shoes line up on the floor, and miscellaneous items are handily stacked on the top shelf. She gives her head a shake and narrows her eyes at her sister, *the perfect twin.*

Brenda ignores that look continuing:

"Oh Gee, what are we going to do now? You know Gran has been wanting us to move back East, she fought with Mom about it all week, and after this, well. But I don't want to go. I know that's where Gran has her life and all her friends and stuff, and it wasn't fair of Mom to just disrupt things and move us all here, but I love it here. I want to stay."

"I hate it here."

"You hate it everywhere."

"True."

"So you might as well hate it here as anywhere else, right?"

"We're seventeen, Bee, I don't think we're going to get a say in the matter."

Grant has visited the victim's house before, in fact he'd had lunch there with the previous owner, and remembers it had an ultra-modern design. On that occasion he'd only seen the front entry and the kitchen but today he went to the upper floor to Barbie Nichols bedroom.

The architect probably considers the staircase a masterpiece but to Grant it's a monstrosity. In a house decorated in shades of gray, with a few black and white accents, the modular curving stairs in a fire-engine red acrylic, is an eyesore. *Damned difficult to walk on, too!* he thinks as he carefully navigates the slippery steps that seem to float they look so insubstantial.

He safely reaches the landing where he notices that access to the second floor up is via a normal set of stairs. That's where the three older kids have their rooms – each with their own en suite bath – and a communal den, according to the constable who's given him the layout of the place.

The hi-tech colour scheme extends to the halls and rooms but Barbie Nichols had imprinted her own style on the master bedroom. Half-a-dozen brightly coloured cushions featuring whimsical cats are scattered on the floor, knocked off of the bed. The bedspread is a violet and aqua mix that shouldn't work but somehow does. It's vibrant, rather than the blinding.

Flowers on the dressers, clothes tossed over a *chaise longue*, a selection of wigs draped over an antique-looking cheval standing mirror rebel against the sleek lines of the glossy black furniture. Lots of electronics too: an Alexa, desktop computer, iPad, wall-mounted flat-screen TV, and a Bang & Olufsen sound system that makes Grant drool.

Two open doors lead to a walk-in closet, rather sparsely occupied, and a full-size 4-piece bathroom. Traces of powder sprinkled on the floor give off a strong smell of honeysuckle from an overly generous application rather than spillage.

A shelf runs around half the bathtub and it's laden with fancy-shaped containers, colourful bottles, many candles, and more flowers. Obviously Barbie Nichols spent a fair bit of time relaxing in the oversized tub. A plush bathmat matches equally fluffy towels folded over a heated rail. A lot of luxury for the late occupant.

Grant considers that sobering thought as he turns to inspect the bed where the body was found.

Covid-19 Update: Evidence now shows the virus isn't as lethal as first believed. Antibody testing indicates about five times more people have been infected but they haven't reported any symptoms. This means the Infected Fatality Rate (IFR) is well below 1%, similar to the IFR of influenza, flu, in a bad year.

Chapter Four

Thursday, April 23, 2020

Grant and Reg are meeting Dr. Alexiy in his office, which Grant vastly prefers to the examining room itself, but the smells linger in every room of the whole morgue. The man arrives still wearing gloves but pulling off his face mask. He examines the article for a moment before muttering obscurely *good thing I'm used to wearing one of these.*

The autopsy report Grant is reading doesn't add any new information – just confirmation of the medical examiner's findings during the postmortem. Full analysis of stomach contents and tox screening are still to come but there is no indication of heavy enough drinking or drugging to render the victim unconscious before the attack.

Grant had already come to that conclusion when he visited the victim's home. Her body had already been removed but he'd seen the rumpled bedclothes at the scene. Studying the many photographs he saw that the bed sheets had been pulled right up to the victim's chin, trapping her arms, and it was only the rumpling of the covers where her hands and feet had lain underneath that showed her struggle.

The doctor opined that the murderer had held the pillow over the victim's face, pressing down with both arms and torso, to still any sounds and to contain the thrashing about. Grant shuddered at the horror of those four minutes or so that she'd suffered through, and from the look on Reg's face he felt the same revulsion.

"For a short time it's possible to breathe through the fabric of the pillow, there's always some air trapped inside, but eventually suffocation occurs," the pathologist explains.

"It would take a fair bit of strength wouldn't it? To hold down steadily while a fit adult woman is fighting against you?"

"If she was asleep when the attack began half the damage would have been done by time she woke enough to realize what was happening. So yes, it would take physical strength but maybe not as much as you'd think. Even more so, it would take great mental stamina to follow through once the struggling began. Off the record I would say the killer felt real anger, even hatred, towards Ms. Nichols."

"A crime of impulse and opportunity?"

Closing the file on his desk the man looks over his glasses saying, with a bit of a smirk:

"That's your job to figure out, Detectives."

"So what's your thinking about suspects?" Reg glances over at Grant from behind the wheel. He's in his comfort zone, relaxed and ready to talk, to speculate and hypothesize.

"Well, for starters there's the family. Within the 24-hour time period up to her death Barbie Nichols had quarrelled with her husband, her stepson, her–"

"Sorry to interrupt, but remind of who's who."

"Right. Husband Greg Nichols, stepson Gary Nichols, her daughter Glenda Nikovics, the *difficult* twin, and her mother, Moira Nikovics. And I just found out about a sister of Barbie's, Bonnie something-or-other – even Moira doesn't know her latest married name – who is flaky, apparently."

"Why would Barbie Nichols' mother and her daughter have the same surname?"

"Because Barbie Nichols wasn't married to the twins' father. Barbie's maiden name was Nikovics so her daughters were assigned that name, the same name as their grandmother who raised them."

"All one big, happy, extended family?"

"No, apparently Barbie dumped them on her mother when they were only infants and she disappeared for years. According to Moira Nikovics, and so far we have no corroboration about this, she and her daughter had always been in touch, but Barbie was never in touch with her children. Apparently she was terrified of their father, and remained paranoid about him for years."

"And he isn't suspect number one because...?"

"He's dead."

"Sure about that?"

"No, but the authorities declared him dead nine or ten years ago, after he'd been missing for the requisite seven years."

"Damn, might have guessed that solution was too easy."

"Oh I'm a big believer in *Occam's Razor*, Reg, but so far there are no clear and likely answers, yet."

"Still, a dangerous abuser disappears and then his wife, or rather the mother of his children, turns up murdered. Unfortunately that's all too common an occurrence. What were the circumstances of the man's disappearance and presumed dying?"

"He's believed to have died of drowning due to hypothermia. He'd been in prison, got released, re-offended right away but escaped custody on his return to jail and fled into the wilderness. They tracked him for some distance but the trail grew cold – no pun intended! – at a lake.

The water in our mountain lakes is really cold all year round because it's fed by glaciers and snowpack. The experts reckon about an hour tops and then hypothermia sets in. Even the best swimmers can't save themselves when their muscles can't move their arms or legs.

The Underwater Search Team, a group of divers – civilians who volunteer – searched but the lake in question, I looked this up, is about 65 metres deep and 21 kilometres long. So even with sonar images it's a difficult place to search.

In the last sighting of... hang on, I made a note of his name, yeah it's Anton Czerny spelled C-Z-E-R-N-Y and I'm probably not saying it right, anyhow the last sighting of Czerny was him in a wooded area on a trail that comes out at this lake and that was like sixteen years ago."

"And you said he'd been in prison so chances are if he did manage to safely escape from that area he would have re-offended sometime in those years and his records would have popped up."

"Another good reason for the presumption of death."

Reg is driving them back to their station and the two men are silent for the rest of the trip, thinking over the inconvenient fact of Anton Czerny's death.

I'm going to spare you the details, they're on the gruesome side," says Grant. He and Judith are sitting together on her couch and he had his arm around her shoulders but has shifted position to take a sip of coffee.

"Gruesome. That's a word you don't hear much these days. Same as ghastly," Judith replies.

"My grandparents kept a few books for me and my sisters at their place and there was one that I loved called *Beastly Boys and Ghastly Girls*, but I don't remember anything about it other than the name. I think it was funny rhymes."

"I never heard of it."

"No, it was an older book and probably no longer carried in the library by time you were learning to read."

"So, to get back to *gruesome*, you realize my imagination is conjuring up horrible images so you might as well just tell me."

"I get what you're saying it's just... well, you knew the woman and you liked her. It's hard to hear facts about her dying without feeling emotional. But, you're right. The truth might not be as bad as whatever it is you're imagining.

It was a bloodless death, of course, and the body had already been removed by the time the locals called me in but the scene showed where the sheets and duvet had been pulled aside in the struggle and it was a very telling scene. I can't explain it any better than that."

"Poignant?"

"Hmm, there's another of those old-fashioned words but yeah, that fits what I was thinking and feeling."

"Thank you for sharing that with me, Grant. I hope you know you can say anything to me, I'm not a fragile woman. I am naive about a lot of things, I know, but I can learn and I'm willing to do so. You've already taught me so much," Judith says with a shy smile.

"We aren't talking about criminal investigation any more, are we?" Grant answered with a smile of his own.

"Well... I just wanted to be sure you knew you could confide. Apparently it's the distancing and lack of communication that causes most police marriages to fail. You'd think it would be the hours but.. Oh! what's wrong, Grant?"

Grant stood up abruptly leaving Judith looking at him in surprise. He's run his hands through his hair, ruining the normally impeccable styling. He's frowning and looks anxious.

"Nothing's wrong, not wrong, but well... marriage, failed marriages, that's quite a leap. Anyhow, Judith I've got to get going. I shouldn't have ducked out today at all, but I did want to see you. I'll try to see you again tomorrow. I guess you're pretty bored stuck home on your own so much, eh?"

Judith frowns back at Grant trying to understand why his conversation is jumping all over the place. Obviously he needs to get going now so she simply stands up to walk him to the door.

"No jacket, right?"

"No, when I left I thought it was going to be nice out, real spring weather, you know? Oh well, it's coming. If I don't get to see you tomorrow I'll call," He gives her a chaste close-lipped kiss but she slips her hand behind his neck and makes him kiss her properly.

"I'm glad you stopped by," she says when they pull apart. He leans in to rest his forehead against hers and they just stand like that a moment, each thinking their own thoughts. He kisses her cheek, her nose, and her lips then says goodbye and leaves.

Judith feels puzzled by Grant's behaviour but shrugs it off as she locks up for the night.

Covid-19 Updates: The few shops that are open, like hardware stores selling essential goods, will not take back any product for any reason. Once the item is in your home it's yours. The utility companies won't come inside either. They leave coils of cable wire at your front door and tell you to just keep what you don't use.

Chapter Five

Friday, April 24, 2020

The neighbourhood of *McMansions,* large homes with only a couple of metres of lawn separating them, soon becomes streets full of real mansions. Huge homes set well-back from the road. Most are fenced-in and some have ornate gates closing the world out. What they don't have are sidewalks, only a shoulder of fine gravel or in some cases, just a boulevard of brown grass between the property and the road.

Moira is the only person out walking today, same as yesterday and the day before that. No one walks here, they don't even jog. No infants in prams or toddlers in strollers, no seniors being pushed in a wheelchair, and no dogs on leashes. There isn't even a bus stop for the hired help to walk to and from. No one walking... except Moira.

With so many people are stuck at home nowadays you'd think they'd enjoy getting out for a breath of fresh air, change of scene, stretch their legs... but no, thinks Moira. Certainly no one else is outside smoking. She hates living here.

Her life in Alberta has always been an unhappy memory for Moira. Widowed too young from a husband she'd deeply loved, raising Barbie and Bonnie on far too little money, and finally the painful violence of Barbie's boyfriend Anton. She'd been happy and relieved to leave it all behind when she moved with her granddaughters to Toronto. There she'd built up a colourful life with her boutique in Yorkville and her lovely home on Avenue Road. A home with character, not like these soulless tributes to wealth.

Barbie winning the lottery is the worst thing that could have happened as far as Moira is concerned. It's caused fights in the family plus jealousy, bitterness, and resentment. It also resulted in Barbie demanding, after all these years, that her daughters be returned to live with their mother. Of course Moira has to come too, after all she's the one who raised the twins, and they are her girls.

As per their regulations the Lottery people demand photos of the winner. Barbie has rushed them all out here in order to play the part of a good and generous daughter, wife, and mother with her loving family gathered round. It was fun and so exciting at first – winning the lottery! Moira knows how her daughter's family struggle with debt and now there'll be no more worries about *how will we afford it if the car breaks down?* or scrimping at the grocery store while waiting for payday, or dodging the creditors phone-calls.

Then there was the shocking number of begging requests – from individuals, charities, schools, churches – Moira has truly been amazed at the vast number of people willing to put pen to paper to ask for money from a stranger. Plenty of sob stories but also many feeling that Barbie should *do the right thing* and share some of her wealth with them. Pleas soon became angry demands followed by vile hate mail and finally the threats of kidnap and of killing.

Once again Barbie's picture will be splashed all over the news but no grins from the family this time – they'll all look sad or grim because of her death.

Is it actually possible that the lottery win enraged some psycho to the point that he'd murder her daughter? The way their world has been turned upside down makes it possible for Moira to believe anything.

Anyone following Reg will think he's just driving aimlessly but in fact the man is alert to his surroundings while noticing and storing up details in his memory banks. He finds he does his best thinking behind the wheel but still, subconsciously, his cop's eye is always looking.

He drives past all of the schools and playgrounds, around the perimeters of the parking lots at the two malls, through the drop-off centre for recycling and donations, and over to The Centre which is bustling with activity as usual. He finishes his cruise with a drive through the trailer park where there had been all that trouble back in February.

In his mind he is considering the possibility that Barbie Nichols' killer isn't a member of her family. What is the likelihood of her murder stemming from a robbery or kidnapping gone wrong? Whenever there's a lot of money there's a lot to lose. The lowlifes are always on the prowl for opportunities. And of course there are always psychos on the loose.

Someone could easily have seen Barbie's picture on the TV news and decided either she was sending him a secret message, or that God/ Satan/Spacemen had ordered him to kill her. The do-gooders on the far left did a lot of damage when they *emancipated* the mentally ill from their incarceration in asylums, and the penny-pinchers on the right were only too happy to shut down the facilities and cross off that expense from the balance-sheet. The result? a lot of people who should be receiving care are wandering the streets without their medication.

When he and Grant discussed the suspect list they considered that the killer might have slain the wrong victim. Barbie Nichols has only lived in this house for a month. From the sounds of it the woman who lived there before was a piece of work, but it's an unlikely supposition. They put that possibility at the very bottom of their list.

The fact that Barbie Nichols has been murdered in her own home and in her own bed argues against a stranger killing. Family was at hand with no excuse required for being there. And use of a pillow makes the crime seem impulsive, but full of hate. A difficult way to die and a very difficult way to kill but no one can *push your buttons* like your nearest and dearest. So yeah, the family members will be under a microscope and while the lottery money is probably the motive they have to keep their minds open to other possibilities. Maybe Barbie Nichols would have died even if she'd stayed poor?

Grant is having a hard time getting a handle on Greg Nichols. For a grieving widower he seems more angry than sad. That's fairly common, the survivor blaming the victim for being in the wrong place or doing the wrong thing or just for leaving them behind. But something's different, off, with Nichols.

Greg Nichols is such an average sort of man. No doubt he's accepted as *one of the guys* at work or the bar, but looking at him right now Grant is struck by the lack of distinguishing features, the bland personality, the physical description that could match most of the population's white men of Greg's particular age. Everyone talks about the vibrancy of Barbie Nichols so this marriage must be a classic example of *opposites attract.*

Or maybe it's just that I don't like the man, thinks Grant, then amends that thought to: *Maybe I'm the problem.*

"Okay, Mr. Nichols let me confirm what you've said so far. You and your wife fought–"

"No, it was just an argument."

"But you stayed out all night, right?"

"Well, I was pissed off and then I got pissed. I wouldn't drive like that."

"No, I expect someone who drives truck for a living has to be especially careful."

"You'd be surprised," mutters Greg Nichols.

"You said that the two of you started fi– uh, quarrelling during dinner and by time you left the house it would have been between 8:00 and 9:00."

"Yeah, something like that. We usually eat at 6:30, 7:00 but now that Barbie isn't out working any more sometimes we eat earlier. It all depends. Oh..." he stops for a moment as the realization hits him again. Grant sees tears in the man's eyes but he gets himself under control.

"So what did you argue over?"

"The usual, money. You know, when we were broke we argued about money – about having no money – all the time so you'd think that now, well everything would be great, right? Not! Seventeen *fricking* million dollars, it's just too much. It changes things, it changes people."

"You're saying that winning the money changed your wife?"

"Oh yeah. Barbie really changed. She'd never been the penny-pinching type, she was always up for a good time and would joke about champagne taste on a beer budget and then she'd roar out a laugh and say *damn good thing I like my beer*. But once she got all this money, it's like it was water running through her fingers."

"You mean she started splashing out," Grant winced at the unintended pun but fortunately Greg Nichols didn't notice.

"Yes and no. She wasn't a pushover, nobody's sob story was going to pry cash out Barbie, but she spent on big stuff. Like that house. She just went out and bought it, never said a word to me. And she paid cash so it all happened really fast."

"You don't like the house?"

"It's not what I planned on. See, I thought we'd get an acreage and build ourselves a nice place. Not too close to anybody, and with great scenic views. Maybe a log cabin, maybe river rock, or cedar you know, something natural."

"And instead you got an ultra-modern home full of granite and marble."

"A house, Detective. Not a home."

"Your wife didn't share the dream of peaceful, rustic living?"

"She said she wasn't about to camp out in a place that was under construction because it would take years to get it all done just right and she couldn't be bothered with the mess and the inconvenience."

"Why would you have to camp out?"

"We had to get move out of our rental. You wouldn't believe how in your face people get when you have a big win. They act like you *have* to share it with them, that you should just be handing out money to anybody who asks. The other two tenants, the neighbours, the local church, the daycare, everybody wants a piece.

We ended up moving into a hotel. Barbie's mother got us a suite under her name so we could hide out. Barbie was mad it wasn't the best hotel in Calgary but it's still a really good, really expensive place. It's where the visiting NHL teams stay but I didn't see any hockey players while we were there."

"I see. You ended your lease where you were renting, moved into a hotel, and then into the Seely home in the Executive Estates. I know the home, I've been there a couple of times."

"So you know what I mean when I say it's not very homey at all. Have you seen that eyesore of a staircase? And the Executive Estates, well... let's just say that's not really our style. We even had a moving company even though we didn't take much. Barbie bought most of the furniture that was in the house and me and my son could easily have packed up the rest in a U-Haul but no way, says Barbie. I told her she shouldn't worry about what the neighbours think because it's not like they're ever going to be friends with us. She didn't like me saying that. But it's true. We don't fit in."

"And there's a whole houseful of you too, isn't there?"

"Yeah, it's me and Barbie..uh, well. My son Gary, from my first marriage, our two girls, Shawna and Sheila, then there's Barbie's teenage daughters, the twins, Brenda and Glenda, and Barbie's mother Moira who raised the twins. So yeah, there were eight of us and we still have tons of room. The family we bought from only had two people, a man and his young girl. Well, I expect there was a wife but she didn't live there any more for some reason."

Grant is non-committal on the subject of Andrea Seely. He still bears her a grudge.

"Can you tell me specifically what the argument was about, please," Grant's words are more of a demand than a question.

"It was a stupid thing, well isn't that always the way? I can't believe those were the last words we'll ever speak to each other but I guess you hear plenty of people say that, eh? Lots of regrets in life."

Seeing Grant's impatient look Greg Nichols hurries to get his story back on track.

"It was actually over something that started before we moved to the new place. See I wanted to get some fitted shelving in for the new garage but I didn't know the exact measurements and I didn't feel comfortable coming over while the Seely's were still living here and I was kinda bitching about it and Barbie's like we'*ll be there in a week, you can wait until then* but I couldn't. The building store was having a sale that was about to end and I wanted to catch it. 40%, that's a really good savings. But Barbie just laughed at me saying *it's nothing, get it through your head that we don't have to be nickel-and-dimed any more, we've got money* and I said *you've got the money, not me.*

Well, that turned into our usual argument with her wanting everything to be different and me having trouble letting go. I mean, I did have to quit my job. I didn't want to but everybody started acting funny. We couldn't even go out for drinks after work without someone going on about how lucky I was and how about a loan. It was easy enough for me to say *that's Barbie's money, it's not mine to give* but then, especially after a few drinks, guys would get belligerent and tell me I'm whipped and I need to let her know who's boss. Some wiseass said I should just cuff her one, to teach her a lesson like, and I'm ha! yeah no, I really don't want to get charged with assault. Besides, Barbie woulda killed me!"

They both stop and think about the unfortunate choice of words, then Grant motions for him to continue. They've already had this conversation, or parts of it, a few times but with each repetition new things come out and Nichols' body language and tone of voice are nuanced. Grant feels he is getting a fairly accurate picture of how day-to-day life has evolved for the lottery winners. For a start, it sounds like everyone now has way too much time on their hands.

"At dinner on Tuesday I mentioned how much more I'd had to spend on the shelving for the garage since I missed the sale and Barbie finally asked what I wanted the shelves for. I explained I needed space to put all my gear for working on the car since I couldn't do it in the warehouse at work any more 'cause of no longer working there, and she's like you can't work on your car in our garage, there's probably something against doing stuff like that in the Homeowners Association rules. Then I'm saying I'll be damned if I'm taking my pick-up to some shop to get an oil change. No way am I paying for something like that, something I've always done myself because it's easy to do. And she got all huffy about it saying no, things are different now and we got to act different, too. So, that's it in a nutshell. That's the kind of stuff we would argue about. Really stupid, I know but there it is."

"We're back to you leaving between 8:00 and 9:00 and going for a drink."

"I drove around a bit first. I really didn't want to see any of the guys, not when Barbie and me had been fighting. Plus they always expect me to pick up the tab when we're out and I can do that, I mean I can afford it now, but that's not the point. It's them just figuring they don't even have to ask, and ordering Jack Daniels, too instead of draft beer like they'd be doing on their own dime. I don't know, it's just... well, as I said, things have changed."

Grant gets up and moves around the interview room. He is finding it hard to be patient with Greg Nichols' rambling account. Grant knows he shouldn't be so impatient, the man is grieving his wife's death after all. And it isn't just a death, it's a murder. Lately though, Grant finds he's easily irritated. Stretching his legs seems to help and when he sits back down his demeanor is much more relaxed. Greg Nichols has watched the detective anxiously, somehow sensing his annoyance without knowing what's caused it. Suspecting it might him delaying telling his story so he hurries to explain:

"So I drove into Calgary and I just stayed on the Ring Road which brought me down to the southwest quadrant. I was in a mostly residential area, not much in the way of taverns, when I spotted the sign for the Indian Casino. I knew I could get a drink in the Hotel part for sure. So I go in and it's a nice place and I have a couple and get talking to some guys at the bar. They don't know me, they don't know anything about the money, we're just regular guys shootin' the shit, like how it should be. Anyhooo next thing I know is me and my new friends have gone over to the casino side."

"Do you have any idea what time it was then?"

"It was after twelve, just a little bit after. I know because one of the guys said he had to get up early for work next morning and it was Cinderella time."

"So you went into the casino, what did you do next?"

"Just kinda hung out. I'm not much of a gambler and nobody was waving around wads a cash to play with or I would have watched him play. I know one of the guys left to go home and another said he was going to play some slots. I just walked around looking at the people and the games and I ended up in the Poker Room. I know how to play poker but I'm not very good at it. I bought some chips and lasted for awhile. No idea how long but I know I had two beers. When I lost all my chips I went and sat on one of the couches, planning to rest a bit before driving home and next thing I know some guy I've never seen before is waking me up and saying it's time for the free breakfast."

"Right, it's a 24-hour poker room," comments Grant.

"Yeah, and a real nice place, too," adds Greg Nichols.

Covid-19 Updates: The closure of movie theatres, live events, pubs and bars, casinos, bingos, etc… means many people are turning to online alternatives like streaming TV and movie channels which might impact entertainment venues even after re-opening.

Chapter Six

Saturday, April 25, 2020

Brian is flipping through the offerings on Netflix while Lila snuggles back into the sofa, comfortable and content. She's nibbling on popcorn and warns him that she'll have the bowl finished before he even picks out a movie to watch.

"Then I'll just have to make some more," he answers with a smile.

"I've heard that this microwave popcorn isn't good for you," Lila remarks.

"Actually it's not the popcorn, it's the bag. It's some stuff they put on it or in it. Something that causes a chemical reaction when it's nuked," explains Beth.

She's standing in the doorway sipping on some frothy concoction she's made with their fancy coffee machine that produces lattes and cappuccinos. Probably other types of coffee too but Lila has never touched anything in the Penner kitchen. In her opinion that would be making herself at bit too cozy in their home.

"What do you feel like watching, Beth?"

The girl takes a step back saying:

"Oh, I'm not watching TV with you two, I just came for a drink. I'm going online to find some friends to game with, not sure what I'm in the mood for yet."

Lila comments: "I guess with the lockdown everyone's having to resort to socializing this way."

"Beth always did so it's nothing new to her. Honey you won't be *in the way* if you join us, you know."

"Oh Dad, you and Lila might want to talk or something–"

"Beth, stop trying to be tactful. You know how I feel about Lila, and she and I have already talked it over. I've agreed to hold back until Lila is ready for the next step. In the meantime we're really good friends who enjoy having you with us."

"That's right, Beth. Never feel like *three's a crowd* or anything like that. I enjoy being here with both of you."

"Well thanks... but I really do want to get together with my friends tonight. By the way, the series *The Blacklist* is good."

"Oh Judith mentioned that. Grant told her about it and she's totally hooked. Lots of action and twists and turns."

"I thought you wanted to watch a movie?"

"Movie or TV show, I'm good."

"Oh well definitely a series, that way you'll have to come back to see the rest!"

"Yeah, just don't you be watching it without me or I'll make you watch the episodes all over again and you can't say a word about what's going to happen."

"Oh I'll totally be giving a running commentary like *oh this part is soooo good* and *you really need to pay attention to what he's saying here* you know, stuff like that."

"I will shove a handful of popcorn in your mouth to shut you up!" Lila threatens him with the popcorn bowl laughingly. Brian takes it from her and grabbing her wrists pulls her up against his chest and settles the two of them in a cozy embrace.

"There, I can hold onto your arms this way and I've still got one hand for the remote. And I've got the popcorn, too!"

He finds *The Blacklist* on the screen and they proceed to watch, sitting easily together, neither noticing when Beth slips out of the room.

After the first episode Brian asks Lila what she thinks about the show.

"I like it so far, and usually it takes me about three episodes before I can get into a series."

"Yeah, I know what you mean. Okay, ready to watch another?"

"Sure, if you hand over the popcorn."

"Ugh, hang on, I placed it out of reach because I couldn't stop eating it."

"It is good, eh? Extra butter flavour."

"And I've got to watch night-time snacking or I'll get a *Dad bod*."

Lila gently prods his waistline saying:

"I don't think you've got anything to worry about yet, Brian. I can feel your six-pack."

"Oh you'll have something to worry about if you keep poking at me like that..."

"Stop it. No seriously, do you have to work out a lot or something? Doesn't your job keep you fit?"

"It does, but I'm getting older and since I can't go to gyms right now I've got to keep an eye on my calorie intake. Nowadays I have to choose between enjoying a tasty snack, like a bowl of ice cream, or relaxing with a shot or two of Crown Royal."

"Whiskey doesn't have calories does it? I thought mix was the problem and you wouldn't add pop to Crown Royal."

"No of course not, it's perfect for sipping and savouring. But it still has calories. I suppose you have one of those super-fast metabolisms and never have to worry?"

"Of course I have to worry, I'm Italian! I live on pasta and rich sauces. Very little sugary stuff though so that helps."

"And the fact that you're ten or twelve years younger than me doesn't hurt either!"

"You keep talking about getting old Brian, what's brought this on?"

"Impatience, mostly. I always wanted to have a bigger family but after Mandy – Amanda – died, well it didn't seem like I'd get the chance. But now.."

"You would want a baby now? You'd be willing to live with diaper changes, feedings in the wee hours, teething, terrible twos... you've already *been there, done that,* would you really want to go through it again?"

"Sure, I mean you'd be the one doing all the work–" He tries to keep a straight face as he says this which Lila sees through, but she keeps up the pretense telling him he's full of macho crap.

"I am, it's true. I'd love to keep you at home barefoot and pregnant."

"I'd love to be pregnant. I've wanted to have a family of my own for so long now."

"I can help you with that," says Brian with a leer.

"Never mind waggling your eyebrows at me, mister!"

"What can I say? I'm a very focused guy. I enjoy a drink, but I don't do drugs or gamble or chase women or overindulge in anything. Really my only vice is that I'm driven and ambitious. Not to make a lot of money but to achieve my goals, to have the life I've envisioned. And I'd love to have children with you, Lila."

His expression is serious and his gaze probing as he looks into her eyes. She stares back and they both enjoy a wordless communication of promise for the future.

"And Beth has told me often enough that she can't wait to be a big sister."

"She's a lovely girl, Brian."

"I know and I'm so lucky. Whenever I think about how I almost lost her–"

Lila hears the emotion in his voice and leaning in gives him a closed-mouth kiss on the lips and a hug. Again they share a moment full of unspoken feelings.

Covid-19 Updates: Travel agents and airlines are dealing with ever-changing rules for every arrival and every destination point. Canadians can get very cheap flights to Europe but on return have to quarantine. Policies established at the end of March have changed several times but violators can still face up to six months in prison.

Chapter Seven

Sunday, April 26, 2020

Judith is relieved to get Pat's phone call. She didn't hear back from Grant after he left and not a word all weekend, either. He's been a bit withdrawn and distant lately. Judith hopes he hasn't caught the virus.

Pat wants to discuss the province-wide lockdown. Edgemont School for Girls was made to close, same as all charter and public schools, by the government on March 16th.

"You're not out of the house, driving or anything are you?"

"Pat I never talk on the phone when I'm driving. Actually though, you'll probably laugh, but I'm luxuriating in a bubble-bath of all things. I mean, who ever had time for this before?"

"Judith I actually baked bread! First time in years and years, in fact long enough for me to forget that when the yeast blends with the water I get all woozy and have to lie down unless I hold my breath while stirring. Anyhow, back to our plans for the school–"

"First though, how are you feeling now? You and Mark are the only people I know who have actually had Covid-19."

"I've fully recovered, but Mark's still a bit wonky. He got it worse than I did, and now we're wondering if he might have that long-haul Covid condition."

"I haven't heard of that, what is it?"

"It seems quite a few people who had the disease and recovered still have lingering effects. The symptoms range through extreme shortness

43

of breath, tiredness, overall weakness, basically an inability to function the way they used to even though they're over the virus. Even when we had it we both felt mostly okay, but then after a week Mark's temperature suddenly skyrocketed. I called the 8-1-1 Healthline and they said to take him to the hospital but there's new rules about that. You get to the hospital and then you phone, they gave me the number to a direct line, when you arrive and wait in the car in the parking lot for instructions. It felt so strange, like we were in some sci-fi pandemic movie or something.

Anyhow, we did what they said and as soon as I called a doctor came right out, all masked and gloved up, and he examined Mark in the car. He told us he wouldn't be admitting Mark because he believed the fever would break that night so it was better – healthier – not to go into the hospital. But if Mark's temperature didn't drop we were to come back again next day. Well, the doctor was right because at some time in the wee hours Mark's temperature dropped down to normal so he avoided the hospital and respirators and intubation and all that horrid stuff."

"But he's still feeling some side-effects?"

"He just doesn't have any stamina. He used to be on the go all the time but now he has to keep taking breaks to catch his breath and rest up. It's been over a month and he still hasn't shaken this frailty."

"Oh, I can't picture Mark like that."

"I know, it's not like him at all. I tease him that he's far more restful to be around now but honestly? I hate to see him this way."

"Does being Black make a difference in the effects of the disease?"

"It might, but nobody knows anything for sure."

"I'm really sorry to hear this Pat. What's the prognosis, what are the doctors saying?"

"Not much. Again, it's all too new. Mark will probably end up being a test case or something. They're learning more about the disease every day and knowledge is being pooled in an international collaboration which is good to know. Johns Hopkins has an interactive map online tracking known cases throughout the world. We check it at least once a day, it's very informative."

"Well tell him I hope he's back to 100% soon."

"I will do so. Meanwhile, we need to discuss the situation at the school."

Judith gives the hot water tap a turn with her foot. She's thinking she should have soothing baths more often.

"Yes! it's unprecedented and the news from both the school board and the province changes daily and they certainly don't seem to be in sync. Parents need to know what's going on."

"Oh I know, I'm hearing from them and from our Trustees. It's frustrating not to have answers. However, what I want to say, Judith, is that I will continue as is until things get sorted and settled but then I'm stepping down. I've decided to retire and am recommending that you take my place."

That news makes Judith sit up so abruptly a bit of sudsy water splashes over the side of the tub but she doesn't even notice.

"What? You're leaving?"

"After getting sick with the virus, and all the worry that that entailed, Mark and I realized it's time to make some changes. As they say *YOLO: You Only Live Once* and we're not getting any younger. Oh listen to me, I'm full of cliches but I guess I'm feeling a bit awkward about this conversation. Not about you," she hastens to add, "You are the perfect choice as my successor and I'm sure the Board will agree, but just talking about retirement well... Actually I've been thinking about it for some time and I finally decided I need to set a date and put this in motion. So, when the new school year starts I'll have my feet up sipping sangria or something with an umbrella stuck in the glass enjoying the discounted holiday rates of the off season."

"I'm not sure if I want your job, Pat. I mean, Principal? that's a big step."

"Judith nobody really wants the job – the prestige, yes, I can certainly see Marta Smith wanting that – but the actual job of dealing with students, parents, boards, government, budgets, isn't exactly a barrel of laughs."

"You're not selling it well, you know!"

"No, but you know what I mean. It's not a glamourous job, despite the title, but you need a change, Judith. You're an excellent Bursar but you've settled into that position and it's time you took on a new challenge. You have the brains and you're not a pushover and that's what's needed to do this job."

"But I'm not qualified as a teacher–"

"You don't have to be for our type of school and besides, we have teachers with less university education than you have."

"Sure, but mine's in accounting."

"And that's an excellent basis for a leadership role. There are too many starry-eyed individuals who think they can just throw money at a problem. Not true! and you know that. You're a sensible, level-headed, intelligent and tough..."

"Oh cool, so when I apply and they ask for my qualifications I just say what? that *I don't suffer fools gladly* and that's my strength and my weakness?"

Pat lets loose with her booming rollicking laugh replying: "Yeah, that pretty much says it all, that's perfect!"

Covid-19 Updates: Police are ticketing people for violating Covid-19 protocols while in public and citizen journalists posting video clips of these interactions have turned sentiment against law enforcement. Homicides, particularly shootings, have increased and domestic violence calls are way up.

Chapter Eight

Monday, April 27, 2020

Brian Penner lifts up his hard hat to wipe the sweat off his forehead. They've put in a busy morning's work. The cool air on his head feels great so he takes the helmet right off and tilts his face up. The temperatures are still cooler than normal for this time of the year but the warmth of the sun is a blessing. After drawing in a couple of deep breaths he opens his eyes to see the new guy watching with a half-smile.

Brian heads over to chat with the man, Andy he'd said his name was, to tell him he's doing a great job. This is a pleasant surprise because Brian very rarely resorts to picking up day labour from Calgary's *Cash Corner.* Lately though the pressures of this virus, causing illness and fear of infection, have negatively impacted the available workforce. Understandably Brian's client has been pushing to complete the project before everything gets shut down altogether.

Andy looks to be Brian's age, early forties, but the men hiring themselves out by the day usually live a rough existence and are often much younger than their appearance. Andy is a tall man with long limbs and a big man's build except he isn't filled out and his clothes hang loosely. But he wants to work and is healthy and strong enough to keep pace with Brian's crew. Of course his men aren't being friendly towards the newcomer. Andy wandered off on his own when they broke for lunch and no one called him over to join them or offered to share their food.

"Andy," calls Brian, walking towards the man, "I can use you again tomorrow if you're available?" Andy nods *Sure* and Brian gestures to him to follow. They get in Brian's pick-up and drive a couple of blocks to a 7-11 where Brian tells Andy to *get a sandwich or hotdog or something* while he grabs coffees and a dozen bottles of water to take back. When his employee shakes his head Brian is firm saying:

"I'm offering to pay for your lunch because I need you to be able to work. If you're going coming back tomorrow ask the hostel or shelter where you're sleeping at to pack you a meal. I can sign a voucher or whatever you need."

Andy doesn't smile but he ducks his head in a quick nod then studies every offering in the snack selection before choosing roast beef and Swiss cheese. Brian is relieved Andy hasn't picked an egg salad sandwich because the odour he carries into the truck is bad enough without adding the strong smell of eggs and mayo.

If Andy does show up tomorrow, he thinks to himself, *I'll hire him for the rest of the week. Assuming he doesn't take today's pay and overindulge, that is.*

"Sorry I didn't get back to you last night, hon. Probably just as well 'cause I wasn't in the best of moods anyhow."

"Last night? I've been expecting to hear from you since Thursday, Grant. But nothing.

"Judith—"

"Is that why you've been avoiding me lately, Grant? because of what you're doing in your job?"

"No, it's not—"

"Oh, I see. So then it *is* a personal issue, hmm? Yeah, I've heard about this sort of thing."

"What are you talking about? I'm not avoiding—"

"Really? and here I thought couples got together – or at least spoke to one another – on weekends. Especially since they don't usually see each other during the week."

"STOP INTERRUPTING ME!"

"Ah, I'm an interruption am I? No worries."

Call ended. Grant stares at his phone wondering what just happened.

Judith isn't sure herself. She didn't even get a chance to tell Grant about Pat's proposal. Sitting in her office at the school she suddenly bursts into tears.

That startles her out of the peculiar mood she's been in. Judith draws a deep shuddering breath and manages to stop crying. She quickly wipes away the evidence but gets up to close the door anyhow. She needs to verbalize and doesn't want anyone to hear her talking out loud to herself.

"I can't act this way, I need to get to the bottom of this – whatever it is." Still standing by the door she starts to pace around the room but immediately starts counting her steps and that distracts her thoughts. "Dammit, I need to get outside."

It's been a cool April this year with temperatures in the low teens but the forecast is better for the week ahead. Judith hasn't put her coat away in the staffroom because she only planned on a quick visit to the school to go through the halls opening doors to check that everything looks okay. She can't concentrate on doing that until after she gets her head clear so she bundles up again and heads outside. There's no one to see or hear her marching around the wet grass on the field quietly muttering her thoughts.

"It's no use pretending everything's okay or normal or fine. It's not. It's got to have something to do with the sex, or maybe this is typical of the dynamics of men and women? I've heard of men pulling back when they start feeling things too deeply and saying they get frightened. I always thought that was one of those excuses that sound good but are meaningless. But what do I know?

The first time we made love, my first time ever, is a blur and mostly unremembered. For a couple of days I'd been expecting that we'd *do the deed* soon, but it didn't happen, and then the next night again it didn't happen, but when it finally did it was spontaneous, completely unplanned. I'd worried over stuff like *who undresses first?* but that wasn't even an issue. I was already in bed wearing a nightie, and it wasn't night time it was morning.

Grant had insisted on watching over me my first night home from the hospital. Like a gentleman he slept on the couch but when he came into my bedroom to check on me next day I just reached out my arms to him and we consummated our... hmm, less than marriage, but more than friendship. Our liaison. And that's pretty much all I recall, other than we made each other happy.

Lovemaking for our second time is a memory I'll never forget. Nothing hazy about that connection, not at all. Grant took charge of everything first by undressing me and lying down with me out on the bed, then setting the pace of our caresses and directing our um... foreplay. He used his body in ways that teased and tormented me in well, extraordinary ways, until I realized that his pale blue eyes weren't icy at all but instead flamed with blue fire. He showed me both gentleness and passion and throughout it all I was bathed in the comfort of how deeply he cared.

I'm having trouble reconciling the man he was then with the man he is now. In the space of a few weeks he's changed, or at least his feelings towards me have changed. I can feel him withdrawing from me and being evasive in our conversations. Is this what people mean by over-familiarity? moving on when there's no more *thrill of the chase?* I didn't feel like I was being used then, but I sure feel like I'm being discarded now.

I can't get Grant to tell me what's going on, but maybe Lila can give me some insights? When I go back inside I'll call her."

Judith is also enjoying the warmth of the sun on her skin. It lightens her mood and she realizes she has to call Grant as well to apologize for hanging up on him. With a sigh she heads back to the school to finish her chores and make her phone calls.

Judith isn't able to reach Lila on the phone but she sends a text asking her friend to call when she gets a chance.

Instead, Lila has dropped in for a rare visit. She doesn't often invite anyone to come to her place because she's very conscientious about taking home Covid germs to her elderly landlady. However as she said, *this is an in-person conversation and I've been looking forward to having it.*

"I know you're a private person, Judith, and lovemaking is the most private act but do you want to talk about it?"

"Oh yes! First of all it was a wonderful experience. Grant is very good, well I have no one to compare him to, but as far as I can tell he does everything right."

"Oooh, I like the sound of that!" Lila teases.

"The first time was good but the second time, oh my! it was great."

The two women collapse in giggles.

"I was just thinking about this earlier," says Judith. Her smile is huge and it's obvious she's enjoying a happy memory in the privacy of her own thoughts.

"That's all I'm going to get out of you, isn't it?"

"Yeah, 'fraid so. I'm very happy but..."

"Uh-oh, why is there a *but?*"

"Because the last couple of days Grant seems to be, I don't know how to describe it – and maybe it's all in my head – but he *seems* to be pulling away from me."

"What do you mean, exactly? Give me an example."

"Okay, well he's a pretty reserved guy but once we got intimate it felt like he was always reaching out and touching my arm or stroking my hair, and kissing me a lot, but now it feels like he's avoiding any physical contact."

"Hmm, could it just be he's really wrapped up in this new case he's involved in?"

"That's what I wondered. I mean, he is very intense when he's focused on something and I guess, maybe, I'm just a bit resentful that his single-minded focus isn't on me. Oh, listen to me I sound like a spoilt child!"

"No, Judith. You're just a woman who is *finally* indulging and enjoying her first sexual relationship. You want him all to yourself right now and that's understandable. I'm really happy for you, hon."

"Thanks, Lila."

"Unfortunately though..."

"Yes I know, and when I think of poor Barbie Nichols, I just can't believe it."

"Have you spoken to him about it?"

"Not really... he did phone but I don't know, I was just in a mood, I guess, because I was snapping at him, wouldn't give him a chance to talk and then I hung up on him. I need to call him back."

"Well, yeah you do."

"I know, I know. I did send a text saying I was sorry and I'd phone later. Lila I'm too old for this nonsense."

Lila just laughed and said that her parents and her grandparents *still* go through *this nonsense*. It's all about being human and being in love.

"So how are things going with you and Brian? You've been seeing him a fair bit, eh?"

"Yes, we have, but just as friends. "

Judith snorts out a laugh and that makes Lila laugh too.

"Seriously, I think things will develop but we're going slow right now, I'm still feeling bruised by... well, you know."

"Yeah, I know. But Brian's friendship helps, right?"

"It does, it really does. Beth, too. I really like being in their company. We watch movies, chit-chat a lot, have a meal, I'm giving her some basic cooking lessons, that sort of thing."

"Wow, if you're sharing family recipes then things are heating up!"

"Oh stop, I'm just showing her my Nonna's way of making spaghetti sauce because it's too expensive to keep buying jars of the stuff."

"I don't know... sounds pretty serious to me," Judith teases.

"If it gets serious you'll be the first to know. Anyhow, I've stayed too long so I've got to go now. It's been good seeing you face-to-face. Keep me posted and I'll do the same."

"Actually, call me later on when you've got some time to chat, okay? It's nothing ominous but I have news I'd like to talk over with you. Today or tomorrow."

" I'm having dinner with Brian and Beth but I'm intrigued! I'll call you tonight for sure, but it might be late if that's okay?"

"Totally fine. It's not like either of us has to get up and go to work in the morning."

Brian Penner is enjoying peaceful contentment watching Lila teach Beth a safe way to quickly chop vegetables. The realization strikes him that it's been a long, long time since he felt this way. He'll be happier if he can claim Lila as his girlfriend soon-to-be wife but he accepts that only time will resolve that situation. Meanwhile he should savour what he has and he does.

Lila is such an attractive woman inside and out. Her personality is vibrant, she has a pretty face and a sexy figure, and her heart is huge.

She has a great sense of humour, too, thinks Brian. He's a few years older and Lila told him with a perfectly straight face that she appreciates him making his move while he's still healthy enough for her to believe he isn't just after her for her nurse's knowledge of gerontology. He quickly looked up the word on his phone then told her she's a sassy brat who should be spanked. Beth then assured Lila that her father had never punished her like that. The face he makes behind Beth's back implies he has different intentions towards Lila who sticks out her tongue at him when Beth isn't looking. Brat indeed!

After they've eaten dinner Beth is excused from kitchen clean up so she can complete her online homework assignment. Chatting while they work Brian tells Lila about Andy, his new day labourer.

"I'd guesstimate he's in his late thirties or early forties and I don't know what caused his downfall, but he's a good worker. I hope he stays clean and sober tonight and is ready for another shift tomorrow."

"Clean and sober?"

"Sometimes people talk about their troubles but usually only when they figure they've got the problem beat. Or if they've accepted that it will never be beat and they need help to abstain forever."

"Oh! I wonder what's happening with AA meetings? I guess they'll just have to limit the number of attendees?"

"I heard there are some online meetings through Zoom or something."

"It seems sad that for some people the advice about *all things moderation* just doesn't apply."

"No, like your friend Judith, she doesn't drink at all, right?"

"That's true, but Judith doesn't have a problem with it, she's never drank, She can't even bear the smell of booze, but that's because her mother was a drunk. I guess I should pretty that up and say *alcoholic*."

"Pretty it up?"

"Well, I have to confess I'm not convinced alcoholism is a disease."

"But you're a nurse!"

"And that means I know what disease looks like. Disease is children born with their mother's syphilis, it's thirty-five-year-old men shockingly keeling over from heart attacks, it's young people battling cancer, and old folks suffering from dementia. Drug addiction, alcoholism, and STDs are largely preventable."

"What about AIDs?"

"Same thing. Infected people know they have it and need to take precautions and to warn their partners about the risk. Same with herpes and other STDs."

"But some people got AIDs from blood transfusions so—"

Lila interrupts saying: "But not these days. Yes, tragically people were given blood from infected donors but blood is thoroughly screened now."

"That's good to know. I don't know anyone that that happened to personally, but I know of a family whose child with leukemia got AIDs from a blood transfusion and they were hounded out of their small town. Everyone sympathized, but no one wanted their kids in the same classroom or swimming pool. Everyone was afraid they would get sick, too."

"Ugh, I can understand both points of view. AIDS seemed to come on the scene so quickly and so dangerously because so many people dismissed it as *only a homosexual thing*, but that was like 40-plus years ago. Brian, our conversation has certainly come a long way from your new employee, and that's probably my fault. If there's a side-road or a byway you can count on me to be racing down it."

"Good to know, I'll keep that in mind when you start to ramble."

"God yes! otherwise I forget the original topic," she laughs.

She's been handing him the dirty dishes and approves the way he's placing them to maximum effect in the dishwasher.

"Well talking reveals so much. I now know that you're pretty inflexible when it comes to self-induced or preventable trauma."

"True, but I'm not unsympathetic, I'm just a bit more ruthless in prioritizing. For example, I was a smoker for years and if I got lung cancer I would know that my actions contributed – probably even caused – the disease. But that doesn't mean I think I, or any other smoker or ex-smoker, *deserves* to get lung cancer. I'm so thankful that I was able to finally quit and I understand the difficulty because I found it really hard. But if I had to choose between a lifetime non-smoker versus a smoker to get a lung transplant I'd go with the non-smoker."

"Isn't that kind of like playing God?"

"No, the issue isn't between young or old, mentally-challenged or brilliant student, male or female, or anything like that, it's between victim of circumstance and victim of risk-taking."

"Wow, I'm seeing a new side of you, Lila."

"Uh-oh, I hope I'm not disappointing you."

"No, not at all. I was just thinking you have like the biggest heart but you're practical with it. I think that's a great way to be."

"I think that compliment deserves a kiss," she says, leaning in. Brian is a wonderful kisser: tender, considerate, and with just the right amount of passion. They kiss for a couple of minutes before Lila pulls back with a smile saying,

"Okay, let's get back to your new employee."

"Who?"

"Ha-ha. Andy."

"Oh yeah him... actually he's not an employee he's just casual labour. A good worker, as I said, but a man doesn't reach his age without some history. What his story is remains to be seen and I might never know. If he doesn't volunteer I sure can't ask."

"Aren't you curious?"

"Sure, but not enough to intrude."

Lila gives an exaggerated sigh saying: "Men!"

Brian leans in close saying:

"I'm perfectly willing to satisfy your curiosity about *this* man–" but Lila interrupts him with a kiss that he returns with passion.

Grant interviews Glenda but the girl is sullen and unresponsive. Big sighs between each answer and then it's only to give a *yes, no,* or *I don't know* response. Glenda is under eighteen so Moira is present, sitting quietly, but eventually she loses patience and tells her granddaughter to *smarten up and just admit she was home all night* .

"I know, I saw you here. You didn't go out."

Grant notices a mere flicker of a glance exchanged between the two. Is Moira protecting Glenda? or giving herself an alibi? More questioning and Moira admits she's the one who went out that night.

"Okay I was out, but just briefly, just 30 minutes... 45 tops, while I walked to the store and then came straight back."

"You walked at night? On a Friday night?"

Moira gives him an amused look as she continues saying:

"No one's going to bother me. At my age the boys looking for trouble aren't interested, and it's obvious I'm not worth mugging."

"But still, it's risky to be out walking on your own at night."

"She has every right to go walking at any time of day. Women shouldn't have to live by a curfew just because men can't control themselves!" bursts out Glenda, showing some animation for the first time. "If it isn't safe for her it's because you're not doing your job."

Neither Grant nor Reg have an easy answer to that accusation but before they can even try Moira responds:

"Well I don't drive so I don't have any choice, do I?"

Choosing to ignore Glenda's outburst Grant asks:

"Where did you go to shop?"

"Just the 7-11, I needed cigarettes. Barbie decided we should all quit smoking and bought those nicotine puffers instead of getting me my smokes. I told her I have no intention of quitting, I *like* smoking, but of course she argued and there's no changing her mind once she's set on something so I just went out and bought them myself."

"So you and your daughter had an argument that evening, and later that night she was killed."

"What are you trying to say!" shouts Glenda on her feet with her fists clenched.

"We're just asking questions, Miss, and we're asking everyone connected to your mother. Your grandmother is answering helpfully but not you. Why is that? Why aren't you trying to help us?" Reg sounds annoyed which surprises Grant. In the short time he's known the older man he's always found him to be easy-going, calm, and professional. He wonders if this is an interrogative tactic?

"I don't have to help you. Stop picking on my gran and stop picking on me!"

"Detective Grant I think we should take Miss Nikovics to the station where we can ask our questions in a formal interview."

"Officer I really don't think that's necessary—"

"I'm sorry Mrs Nikovics, but I think it is. Glenda is being obstructive and her answers are evasive. Maybe she'll take the questioning seriously when she's under caution and on tape and video. We would like you to come with us, too, as Glenda's legal guardian." Both men have stood during Reg's statement and are now waiting on Glenda, who is looking defiant, and Moira who is exasperated with her granddaughter.

"You'll have to drive us then, she's only got her Learner's Permit, well had it.. anyhow, she can't drive at night."

Grant suppresses a smile when he replies:

"Yes, we were planning to drive you. And, of course, we'll bring you back home afterwards."

Reg has started the police car while Grant gets the two women settled in the back seat. He is just getting in himself when a Smart Car with an Uber sticker draws up alongside them on the driveway. Brenda Nikovics jumps out crying:

"What's going on? Where are you going?" and turning to Grant asks: "Where are you taking them? and why?"

Grant explains that Glenda was going to the police station to answer questions and gets in the passenger seat, closing the door in Brenda's shocked face. He sees her rush back to the Uber and get in it again, obviously directing the driver to *follow that car!*

It's late when Lila phones Judith and they've barely gotten past their *Hellos* when Judith says:

"Oh, hang on. There's my buzzer. I can't imagine who it could be at this time of night, I'm not expecting Grant but... Hold on while I check," Judith presses the *Talk* button on her intercom saying "Hello? who is it?" then she presses *Listen* and hears a young, desperate-sounding voice in tears crying:

"Oh Miss Taylor, I really need your help. It's Brenda Nikovics and something terrible has happened with my sister, Glenda. Can I talk to you?"

"Yes of course, I'm coming down now," answers Judith, grabbing her keys and hurrying out the door. "Did you hear all that, Lila? I don't think you've met Brenda, she only just came to the school when she moved into her mother's new home. I know you know about her mother being found murdered–"

"Yes, but now it sounds like the problem is with the sister. Judith, deal with this and call me back as soon as you can."

They disconnect just as Judith comes into the lobby to let the distraught teenager inside. She flings herself into Judith's arms and is awkwardly held while she sobs. Judith leads the girl back up the stairs to her place but only long enough to grab her coat and purse. As they head back down the stairs to the parking garage Judith instructs Brenda to tell her everything.

"The police have arrested Glenda, my twin, for killing Mom but she didn't do it and you have to help me convince them."

"Me? but I don't even know Glenda and–"

"No, but you solved cases before, I heard all about it at school, and you know the policeman in charge. We don't know anybody, Miss Taylor, you're my only hope!"

Covid-19 Updates: The province recommends restricting your household to family members only, but if essential visitors need to come in they should stay no more than 15 minutes. Both indoor and outdoor gatherings are only allowed limited attendance. Violations can result in a $1,000 fine.

Chapter Nine

Tuesday, April 28, 2020

"I don't mind a long conversation on the phone," begins Lila, "but I'd love to get out of this place for a couple of hours. What are we allowed to do?"

"We can pick-up coffees or food to go so long as we stay back six feet and use sanitizer when we enter and when we leave."

"I could go for a pizza, what about you?"

"Sounds good, but where will we eat it outside? We're not allowed to sit at picnic tables or on park benches and all the playgrounds are shut down."

"The school! We can go sit on the steps round back. They don't face the road so no one will see us. They won't even see our cars in the staff lot."

"That will work. I'll grab the pizza, you get coffee and doughnuts."

Division of labour sorted, the women, happy to get out of their homes for a while, complete their tasks and meet up as planned.

Judith keeps a blanket in her trunk – along with other breakdown-in-cold-weather supplies – so she lays that on the steps and they spread out the food.

"This is delicious pizza," says Lila around a mouthful.

Judith laughs and answers: "You had a great idea."

They eat their lunch and finish with a coffee and dessert.

"I want to start with my story, mine and Pat's, and then I'll tell you what happened with Brenda."

"Last night's text was reassuring, especially now that there's no urgency."

"Yeah, sorry about not calling but I was just too tired to talk any more."

"Never worry about sending me a text!" Lila chuckles, "Believe me, it's my preference."

"Anyhow the original conversation I wanted to have with you like 24-hours ago? is that Pat is going to retire and she wants to nominate me as her replacement."

"Wow, I'm really surprised about Pat retiring, but not wow that she's choosing you as her successor. That makes perfect sense. I mean, you're Acting Head now and you've handled that job several times in the past. Even during a murder and kidnapping investigation, so that's a no-brainer. But why is she retiring?"

"I think them getting sick with Covid was like a wake-up call or something? Like a *this is it, this is all you get for a life so make the most of it* kind of thing."

"Is she even 65 yet?"

"I don't think so, but I'm not sure. Mark is past 65, I remember when he had his retirement party–"

"You went?"

"God no, all those strangers? Not a chance."

"That's the Judith I know–"

"And that's the problem," Judith interrupts in an anxious tone of voice. "I'm not sure I should even consider applying for the position of Principal. It's such a people-oriented job and dealing with people is not my forte."

"How do you know?"

Judith gives Lila a quizzical look as if to say *that's a stupid question.*

"I'm serious. You've never really given yourself a chance. I'm not blaming you, avoiding and even hiding away from people because of mother's problem–"

"Alcoholism."

"Yeah, okay, your mother's alcoholism was a fact of life for you growing up, but now? who knows what you can do?"

"But I don't even like people and I can't talk to them."

"Of course you can! I watched you handle a difficult school assembly and a parents' meeting and both times you were *calm, cool, and collected.* Judith you just need the confidence to spread your wings."

"I didn't have a choice about either of those things, it just had to be done."

"And you stepped up to do it and you did it well. You have natural poise and an air of authority. Besides, you know Marta Smith will want the position so you have to take it. I can't possibly have her as my boss."

"Eww, you're right. I'd report to her as well. Oh, she'll really hate it if I move up from Acting to Permanent Principal. Hey, if I get the job maybe that will finally push her into retiring!"

"Well I think that's being a little optimistic but who knows? Anyhow, Pat thinks you're the right choice and so do I. What does Grant say?"

"Pffft. I haven't told him yet, we haven't spoken at all. I'm annoyed at him for frightening those girls, imagine arresting a teenager for matricide."

"Right, but he didn't actually do that, did he?"

"Well, no. Brenda got the wrong end of the stick there... but he really gave her a scare. That much is true."

"What exactly happened?"

Judith goes on to relate how she'd brought Brenda up to her apartment but only long enough to grab her purse and a jacket. Entertaining a student in your home was an absolute no-no, no matter what the reason, so she'd ushered the girl down to the parking garage to drive her home.

"I'd once driven Margaret Seely home so I knew the house but couldn't remember what street it was on. Brenda gave me directions but said she didn't want to go home, she wanted to go to the police station. I had to explain that I couldn't possibly take her there at that time of night. The only place we could go was to her home but we could sit in the car in the driveway to talk if she didn't want to go indoors."

"Your text said Glenda was already back home when you got there."

"Yes, thank goodness. Of course we didn't know that, not until Glenda came outside. Then it was tears of joy and twin-speak. At least that's what I call it – when they talk to each other but half the words are left unsaid? Anyhow, I still don't know the whole story of what happened. I guess I do need to talk to Grant."

"Yeah, I think so."

Lila stands and starts packing away the garbage while Judith folds up her blanket.

"I'll take that stuff," she says, adding that there's a dumpster at her building.

"Brenda did say something that only struck me as odd later on, I wish I'd asked her to explain but..."

"What was it?"

"Well, I was trying to make conversation during the drive, you know something to distract her from her worries and her crying. Anyhow, I asked how she and Glenda liked being here, in Edgemont. She's a smart girl because she answered that she appreciated me trying to make her feel better, but I didn't need to. Then she went on to say:

Everything is great, she loves her home, her school, her family is wonderful, and once they get past the jealousy it will be perfect. After all, it's only natural that they want to spend time with their mother and same with her buying them presents, they've never lived together before so yeah, they're enjoying most of her attention and that's normal. It won't last forever, some people just need to learn patience."

"Huh! I see what you mean because who was she talking about? The grandmother might be jealous that the girls want to spend time with their mother, the husband might be jealous that she was spending money on them, her siblings might be jealous about the attention the twins are getting... but they're too young to do anything. Hmm, I wonder who needs to learn patience? Could it be jealousy between the twins themselves?"

"I don't know. I wish I'd asked her to be specific."

They walk to their respective cars but before getting in Lila says:

"So, *One:* you're going to tell Grant about Pat's offer and we know he's going to support you so can then call her to say you'll accept; *Two:* you'll find out what happened with Glenda and why Brenda thought she'd been arrested, and who is jealous?; and *Three:* you're going to let me know what everyone said, right?"

Judith sighs deeply but agrees to Lila's plan.

"Well there's no time like the present so go take care of business."

Lila gives her a wave and drives away in her sporty little car. Judith remains for a moment longer looking back at the familiar brick building that is Edgemont School for Girls. She's worked there for a number of years but is now looking at it with different eyes and from a viewpoint of much more responsibility.

"So do you have family in the area? or know folks from 'round about here?" asks Brian.

"My girls," replies Andy. "But I don't see them. I'd like that to change, though."

"Is their mother keeping them from you?"

"No, she's not a problem. Not now. She's with another guy and she's been married to him for years. No, the problem was me being unable to settle down and travelling around a lot. I did stay put in Banff for a few years, but it was just a menial job I was doing. Living there, enjoying the scenery and the outdoors, made up for the boredom of the work but in the end I gave it up."

"So your girls live in Calgary?"

"Mmm. I'm not sure there's a place for me in their lives after all this time. I'm still trying to decide if I should even bother."

Brian nods, but realizes Andy's lack of detail and sidestepping of the direct question means he doesn't want to continue the conversation. Tactfully, he changes the subject.

"I'm having a barbeque at my place. Just a few of the single guys because we aren't allowed to have many people at gatherings, right? and you're welcome to join us."

"A backyard barbeque with a few guys sounds really good... great, actually. Thanks."

"Where the hell is Gary?" demands Greg as he comes stomping into the kitchen and interrupting his stepdaughter's conversation with their grandmother. The three women just look at him and when he doesn't give a word of apology Moira just shakes her head, saying:

"I haven't seen him and we *were* having a conversation here, a private conversation."

Hearing their father's voice the two younger girls come in and soon the kitchen is crowded with women all talking at once. At least that's how it seems to Greg who is suffering with a hangover. He can't complain though, he was out with his friends and who does that when their murdered wife isn't even in her grave yet? It's not like he was drowning his sorrows although that was the original pretext for the trip to the bar.

"Gran are you going to stay here and take care of us like you did with the big girls?" asks Shawna, her voice a bit whiny. Before Moira can reply the girl continues: "Daddy can't look after us, even if he is at home all the time now. And Gary's always here, but we don't like him, do we Sheila?"

Her younger sister is busy nibbling the skin around her thumbnail and giving that task all of her concentration. She's chewed the area raw and will soon draw blood which will give her the excuse to suck on her thumb without being reprimanded that at eight years of age she is far too old to be thumb-sucking. She knows all that, but her mother's death and everything that's been going on these past few days have given her plenty of reason to need comfort.

"Why don't you like Gary?" asks their father, clearly surprised at this statement. He would never admit it out loud, but personally he finds his son to be a non-entity, too boring to be offensive.

Brenda leans forward and takes hold of the youngest girl's hand, pulling it away from her mouth and drawing Sheila into a hug. Shawna gives her sister and her half-sister a scowl. She wants the focus of attention to be on herself. It's no fair being stuck in the middle between much older twins and the baby of the family. Gary doesn't count because he's a boy.

"I don't like him 'cause he doesn't like us. He never hangs out with us, he just stays in his room and we aren't allowed in there. It's not fair."

Those last three words punctuate almost every utterance Shawna makes. Her life is just one inequity after another. There is no justice in this world for eleven-year-olds.

"So he's in his room now? I knocked but he didn't answer and I didn't hear anything."

"No, he's not there now. Or... I don't think so but I'll got look, okay?"

"Fine, fine." The unspoken words *just go!* hang in the air. Greg rubs at his temple trying to stave off a headache he feels lurking.

"Come to think of it," says Moira, "I haven't seen Gary for a couple of days now. What about you girls?"

Brenda doesn't hesitate, saying: "Nope, I must have seen him at some point over the weekend but I don't remember when."

"Well, we were a little preoccupied, what with me getting the third degree at the police station," replies her twin.

"What, again?" Greg winces at his own raised voice.

"No, just the one time–"

"Oh, that was hardly an interrogation. God, girl you do love to dramatize, just like your mother does..."

The ensuing silence is uncomfortable but no one rushes to break it. Each reflects a bit on their missing wife, mother, daughter. The sound of Shawna's feet flying down the stairs brings them each back to the here-and-now.

"He's not in his room and his bed hasn't been slept in, not for days," Shawna announces with a ghoulish flourish.

"What? How would you know that?" demands her father.

"Because the bed is made and Tilly hasn't been here since last Friday."

"But Friday's almost a week past!" exclaimed Greg. "Where has he gone?"

"It could even be more than that because I remember the last time I saw him and that was on Wednesday."

"You haven't seen him since a week Wednesday? are you sure, Glenda?"

"Of course I'm sure! we had a fight."

"What about?" asks Shawna, all curiosity, while Greg asks the same question angrily.

"We fought about him being in my bedroom stealing my money."

"What?! No way would he do that!" insists Gary's father.

"I'm afraid so, Greg. He stole out of my purse, too. We caught him and we quarreled about it," adds Brenda in a gentler tone.

"He had no business being in your bedrooms and no right to be taking money from you girls!" says Moira indignantly.

"But why would he?" Greg is sounding plaintive.

"He said he had to get away, to run away before the police arrested him."

"Oh for godsakes why would the police arrest Gary?"

"Because he and Mom had a big fight. He said she kicked him out."

"Oh this is crazy, running away just makes it look worse!"

"Greg, we're going to have to let the police know. They'll have to find him and bring him home."

They all exchanged looks before Shawna asked in a high-pitched voice:

"You mean he killed Mom? I told you I didn't like him."

Covid-19 Updates: Meat-packing plants are suffering viral outbreaks but the forecast of more than 400 in hospital by this date is, thankfully, way off with just 82 hospitalizations, 21 in intensive care.

Chapter Ten

Wednesday April 29, 2020

Judith sends Grant a text inviting him over for dinner. Actually what she's written is:

Judith: made a stew, ready whenever u get here

and Grant replies right away with the thumbs-up emoji and

Grant: 7ish???

but Judith doesn't bother to reply. She doesn't want to look eager. In fact, she's already a little annoyed with Grant and they haven't even spoken yet. She doesn't like the way she's been feeling: anxious about him, about their relationship, and now this job offer... not even an offer, just a proposal to put her name forward. Her getting the school presidency isn't a sure thing.

Oh great, she thinks, *now I have something else to worry about, just what I wanted!*

Lila has just eaten a huge meal of borscht, roast pork, perogies and cabbage rolls all prepared by her elderly landlady. She's still chuckling remembering the expression on Mrs. P's face when Lila asked: *No Chicken Kyiv?* Lila is quite certain she'll be served that dish within the week.

Putting a coffee pod in her machine she calls Brian who answers right away.

"My landlady has fed me so much food I can hardly move! I am so stuffed."

"Wish I'd been there, I love an authentic Ukrainian meal."

"Oh I have leftovers, and pretty much enough to make up a dinner for the three of us. You've got the barbeque tomorrow so we'll have these on Friday night."

"Looking forward to that! We'll probably have leftovers after tomorrow as well. Lots to look forward to, especially to seeing you, as always, Lila."

"That's sweet. Anyhow I'm curious, did your new guy Andy show up again for his third shift?"

"He did, and he worked just as hard as the last few days. I'm still not sure if he'll want to sign on with us, he hasn't said anything about that, but I definitely will hire him."

"And still no idea why he's picking up cash work?"

"Nope. It might not be addiction issues, though. Some of these guys owe a lot of money which they either don't want to pay – like to an ex, – or they can never pay it so they don't even bother trying and just drop out."

"Plus the mentally-challenged, some of whom shouldn't even be on the street–"

"And some who are perfectly capable – and willing – to put in a good day's work but their personal hygiene and clothes keep them from getting a job."

"I thought the shelters had programmes at their facilities for showers, shaving, grooming, even new clothes, to help people get back into the workforce?"

"They do, and they do a good job, but the shelters fill up quickly."

Sighing, Lila comments that it's all very sad, and Brian agrees adding that it's also very common in the cities these days.

"But you'll get to meet him and decide for yourself because he accepted my invitation to the staff party."

Lila is pleased to be helping Brian host this party for his workers. She's wondering what he'll be like and how he'll treat her when everyone is watching how they interact. Is he the type to show her off? or act all possessive? She's looking forward to finding out.

"Detective?" the speech is hesitant but Grant recognizes Moira Nikovics from her raspy smoker's voice.

"Yes, Grant speaking, and it's Ms. Nikovics, isn't it?"

"It is. I'm glad I got hold of you but I can't talk for long. My..." she pauses, thinking, then continues saying: "My son-in-law, Greg Nichols, he didn't want me to call but his son, Gary, is missing."

"How long has Gary been gone?"

"Well... we're not sure but... well, days apparently."

"I'm on my way–" Grant begins, but Moira interrupts asking:

"Can you please not tell Greg that it was me who called you?"

"No worries. I'll see you all shortly."

Ending the call Grant looks up to see Judith's worried expression.

"I guess you're able to piece that together from what you heard. Do you know Gary Nichols?"

"No, I've never met him and I'm not even sure if I've ever seen him... oh wait! yes, once but just from a distance. He was standing outside Barbie's car while she came into the school to pick up Brenda. He was having a cigarette but quite openly, not trying to hide it or anything."

"The grandmother... well, she's not his grandmother, but she's a heavy smoker, too."

"Barbie was as well. I've never seen or smell tobacco on the girls but I don't know about Glenda, the other twin."

"I'd like to discuss her further with you but I've got to go now. Ms. Nikovics is concerned about her Greg Nichols finding out she called us. I think I'd better head over there right away."

Grant is walking towards the door as he speaks but stops and turning asks: "Can I come by later?" and seems very surprised when Judith answers:

"No, not tonight. We'll talk again," and then she is opening the door and giving him a polite smile as she stands well out of reach.

Grant wants to stay and try to figure out what's wrong with Judith but work has to take precedence. He calls up Reg who says he can be at the Nichols' home in the Executive Estates in about ten minutes. The older man is waiting on the driveway, his car parked on the street, when Grant arrives. After quickly bringing Reg up to date the two men head to the front door and ring the bell. It chimes.

"They could do with a roof overhang here," comments Reg looking up. "Especially in winter, or when it's raining."

"That would ruin the *clean, spare lines of the house*," remarks Grant dryly. Reg just snorts a soft laugh.

The older of the two youngest girls pulls the door open saying:

"Yes?"

Grant has heard an urgently whispered *You're supposed to ask who is it first!* and spots the youngest girl hovering behind her sister.

"Sheila is absolutely correct, Shawna, especially at night," he says. Both girls just gape at him but Shawna recovers her belligerence and demands to know *how did Grant know their names?*

"I'm a detective," he replies with a straight face. He hears Reg's cough poorly attempting to disguise a guffaw.

Faced with the two big men the girls step back. At that point Moira Nikovics comes into the hallway, nervously asking what their business is. Grant catches a glimpse of shadow in the room she just came out of and figures they are all being watched and listened to.

"Mrs. Niko..."

"Nikovics."

"Yes, pardon me. I'm here to speak to the teenagers, all three of them please."

"Why? What can they tell you?" she asks but before Grant can answer Greg Nichols step through the doorway saying:

"Gary's not here, and I'm not sure if the twins are around. What do you want to see them about, anyway?"

"That's police business, Mr–"

"Uh-uh, they're teens. You can't talk to them without one of us present."

"Your son has reached the age of majority, Mr. Nichols. We don't need your permission."

"But the girls–"

"Are apparently orphans. I can ask Social Services to appoint an *Appropriate Adult* if you aren't willing to work with us, Ms. Nikovics."

She waves her hand at him exclaiming that of course she will co-operate with the police, they are investigating the death of her daughter.

"And your wife!" she snaps at Greg Nichols who sighs and gestures for everyone to come inside. They all move into the living-room although Greg and Moira try to shoo the two girls upstairs.

"We should stay here, Gran," insists Shawna, "We might know something important, right Sheila?"

The younger girl doesn't give any indication she's even listening but Shawna continues undaunted:

"We might know the fact or find the clue that cracks this case wide open!" she says with excited relish.

"Shawna, stop that!"

"If you must stay then sit down and keep quiet. The sooner the police finish here the quicker they can be out there looking for the bad man who hurt Mommy," says Greg, emphasizing *out there.*

"You mean the killer who murdered our mother," comments Glenda, coming into the room with Brenda just a step behind. They seat themselves on the love-seat with Sheila choosing to sit on the floor between their legs. Shawna perches on the arm, alert and not in the least bit chastened by her father's words.

Seeing the identical twins together Grant is struck by how their attitudes let him differentiate between them. On Glenda her dark colouring, emphasized by Goth-style make-up, gives her a tough, bad-tempered look. Her poor posture and dark clothing add to her sullen, disinterested air. But Brenda's dark hair bounces with waves that catch the light and her dark eyes sparkle. Her good-natured smile shows white teeth set off by soft red lipstick, and her sallow skin is brightened with blusher.

"What time did Gary leave?" ask Reg and Grant gave him a mental thumbs-up for not asking the easier-to-answer *Where did he go?* Now Greg is put on the defensive.

"I don't know, he's a kid always going out and about..."

"You didn't speak to him before he went out?"

"No, no I didn't get the chance..."

"When is the last time you spoke to him?"

"Look what are you getting at?"

"Getting at?"

"Well, with these questions and your tone and your insinuations..."

"I apologise if you find my tone offensive Mr. Nichols, that's certainly not what I want, and I'm not sure what mean by *insinuations?*"

"Well, asking questions like I'm supposed to know the answers and if I don't know then why don't I? it's like you're implying something."

"Hmm," Reg ponders a moment as if giving Greg's half-hearted complain serious consideration. "First, if that's how I sound to you then please let me apologise again. Secondly, if I *do* seem to be implying something's wrong then I guess I must *think* something is wrong. Like, why would Gary leave without touching base with at least somebody, I mean as you said, Ms. Nikovics, this is a murder investigation. Gary's step-mother has been murdered and her killer is still on the loose. I think concern for Gary's whereabouts and well-being *should* be a priority, don't you?"

"Well yes, of course, but he hasn't been abducted or anything–"

"How do you know?"

"Well, why would he be? I mean..."

"When is the last time you saw Gary, Ms. Nikovics," cuts in Grant as he turns to the woman. "You're probably in the house and aware of who else is here more so than any of the others."

"I've been thinking about that, ever since Greg asked me, and I don't remember. But the girls said they last saw Gary to speak to on Wednesday."

"Wednesday! that's a week ago. Do you mean to say no one has seen Gary in a week?" he looks from one face to the other and sees evasiveness tinged with shame.

"We might have seen him but not spoken to him. Or we might have heard him in his room. I just can't remember," explains Brenda.

"Yeah, like we've kinda had a lot on our minds, eh? You know, Mom dying, and catching Gary stealing money from my room, and me being dragged down to the police station..."

"Dragged? Ms. Nikovics?"

"Well, that's how it felt,"

"And what were you saying about Gary stealing your money?"

"That was a misunderstanding, Officer. Glenda, you've got to be careful with what you're saying in case you give somebody the wrong idea. Gary wasn't stealing."

"Taking it without permission and then trying to cover his tracks so he wouldn't be found out? Hmm, sounds like stealing to me." Glenda turns sullen and doesn't want to speak anymore.

Grant decides not to push it. The room is already filled with tension and it's late for the younger girls to still be up. Turning to Reg he asks if he can get things in motion at the station and gets a confirming nod in return.

"I'll head back there now and get started on the Missing Persons report. I'm thinking I should date it *last seen Wednesday April 22nd*, agreed?"

Before Grant can answer Greg Nichols once again intervenes, trying to downplay his son's disappearance:

"It probably hasn't been a week, that's just all we can remember. The girls remember Wednesday because of the incident... the mix-up, that's all. I bet we've all seen him since but just can't remember because it was normal, nothing remarkable."

Grant shares his look from one face to the next until he'd checked in with everyone as he asks:

"Have you seen Gary since last Wednesday?"

No one replies.

Covid-19 Updates: A second state of emergency has been declared in Fort McMurray because of flooding from ice jams forcing thousands to evacuate. Emergency protocols are in place for the weather and the virus.

Chapter Eleven

Thursday, April 30, 2020

It's perfect weather for an outdoor get-together. There's enough of a breeze to keep most of the mosquitoes away and the smoke from the firepit takes care of the rest.

Judith and Lila arrive together, Judith having driven them both. She knows Brian will see that Lila gets home safely.

Although it's only a small group, due to the regulations about gatherings, it's all men which makes Judith draw back, feeling shy, but Lila marches right into the group giving greetings and asking for introductions. Her bubbly social manner puts everyone at ease and there are smiles all round. Judith nods hello here and there knowing she'll never remember all the names. It doesn't matter, she won't be initiating any conversations.

She just gets seated when a tall man, a few years older than herself, asks what he can get her to drink offering beer or wine or... but just then Beth calls out:

"Ms. Taylor, Judith, I've made you some lemonade."

"Oh that sounds lovely, Beth, thank you," then turning to man she adds: "I don't drink alcohol so it's very considerate of Beth to accommodate me."

"I don't drink either!" he exclaims. "By the way I'm Andy, and you are Judith, did she say?"

"Yes, Judith Taylor. Pleased to meet you, Andy."

He looks at her expectantly and then Judith notices he's holding out his hand to shake so she quickly takes it with a nervous smile.

Andy's answering smile is a bit more calculating. He sits in the next lawn-chair and scoots it closer to hers. This allows him to speak in a lower voice that makes their conversation seem far more intimate than it is. Judith is slightly taken aback, she isn't used to men paying attention to her because she isn't used to socializing period.

She gives him a quizzical look and says uncertainly: "We've met before... haven't we?"

"Oh, I would never forget meeting you, Judith. Maybe you saw me in passing? At a mall, a bank, driving by in your car?"

"Maybe.. I don't remember meeting you, but you look awfully familiar."

"Ah, perhaps you saw me and liked what you saw?" He laughs pleasantly and Judith blushes in answer.

Lila looks on with amusement having already noticed that Andy is quite a good-looking man. She begins to wonder what Grant will think of the cozy tableau the two of them make. *If he shows up,* she thinks with a frown.

"What's up, hon?" Brian is right there, spotting her sour look. He follows her gaze to where Andy is monopolizing Judith. Turning back to Lila he asks: "Is that a problem?"

"Oh no, " she smiles. "I'm just being a troublemaker, but only in my own mind! speculating about how Grant will interpret that little *tete-a-tete.*"

"Ahhh, well I know what I'd be thinking if I were him."

"Boy, you sure know how to throw a party, eh?"

"That I do," Brian chuckles, adding: "The secret is to let the guests create their own fireworks."

Once the food is ready to dish up Andy makes a point of helping Judith fill her plate by reaching, fetching, suggesting, and serving. Lila looks on with an amused smile noting Judith's slightly shell-shocked expression. Andy is coming on strong but with extreme courtesy which makes it hard to dissuade him. Along with plenty of compliments, something Judith isn't used to hearing.

Both Brian and Lila exchange a smile when they overhear Andy say:

"But of course you have to have to dessert! With your slim figure you can have two. No need for you to count calories, you are perfect as is!"

And Lila almost laughs out loud when she sees a square of carrot cake and a slice of lemon meringue pie on Judith's plate.

Brian spent quite a bit of money on the party by buying good quality meat for the grill and ready-made fixings – including a variety of desserts. He is in charge of the barbeque while Lila and Beth fetch cold drinks and circulate among the guests. Everyone is having a good time and complimenting their host for picking the perfect day.

Grant spots Judith the moment he arrives but she is engrossed in her conversation and doesn't notice him. She had been glancing at the gate into the backyard with some frequency earlier on but once the meal was served she'd stopped looking, having given up on Grant coming to the BBQ. She certainly understands that his work has to come first and that means it will get in the way of social engagements and she's okay with that. She isn't so sure about the coolness that she's felt entering their relationship, though.

Andy is aware of being watched. Looking up he catches Grant's eye right away and senses antagonism. When Judith follows his gaze her face breaks out in a spontaneous grin and Andy finds himself resenting the newcomer. Grant isn't the type to expect Judith to jump up and fix him a plate, but he does think of her as his lady and is somewhat disconcerted when all he gets is a big smile as acknowledgement.

Lila smooths over the awkwardness with an enthusiastic greeting while drawing Grant by the arm to see Brian at the BBQ and Beth at the tables spread with food. Grant knows both of them and they quickly settle into a *Sorry I'm late* and *Glad you could make it* conversation before commenting on *so much food! great weather! everyone is looking well...* and then *quite a crowd, who is that talking to Judith?*

Brian suppresses a smirk at Grant's poorly disguised rivalry. He and Lila don't really discuss their friends much, they are more her friends than his, but he knows something has been going on... some rift between Grant and Judith. He doesn't know the details, but Brian is sure Grant is a jealous man, even if he keeps his feelings well-hidden.

It was Grant and Judith together who had delivered a big bottle of expensive Scotch to Brian as a thank you for rescuing Judith from an attacker. Brian knew then that while Grant truly was grateful he also resented the other man's heroism, thinking he should have been Judith's knight in shining armour. *And so he should have!* thinks Brian even though the thought is unreasonable. He understands where Grant is coming from.

Now the man is trying to be nonchalant while focussing, intently, on the man leaning possessively over Judith's lawn chair.

"Oh that's Andy, one of my workers. Good guy. He just recently joined the crew and hasn't really made any friends yet."

Again he has to struggle to keep a straight face when Grant snorts over that *friends* comment. Beth has filled up a plate and Grant takes it from her with absentminded thanks. He forks up the food without paying attention to it, his eyes never leaving Judith. She tilts her head and gives him a quizzical look. Grant immediately closes the distance between them and bending down kisses her lips. He looks at Andy who introduces himself but with one hand on the back of Judith's neck and the other holding a plate of food Grant simply nods, unable to shake the man's hand. Grant feels a moment's satisfaction when Andy narrows his eyes, insulted by the Grant's casual behaviour.

"Sorry I'm late but I got held up on the Nichols case, otherwise I'd have been here much sooner." Grant doesn't even bother to include Andy in the conversation. That courtesy falls to Judith who says:

"No worries, I know you're busy. Andy has been keeping me entertained, and fed! He keeps fetching me different things to eat," she laughs. "I've had two desserts!"

Standing over by the grill Brian is occupied talking to a couple of the men so it is Beth who Lila shares her giggles with.

"What's going on?"

"Well, Judith does not flirt – not at all – she's always 100% upfront and sincere, she doesn't hold back. Right now, even though she's not being coy the way she's acting is pushing Grant's buttons and she isn't even aware of it. Most women would be playing it up, flattered by the attentions of two men, but Judith just doesn't think that way."

"But Detective Grant is her boyfriend, right?" asks Beth.

"Oh yes but lately Grant has been living up to his name..."

Beth looks puzzled before bursting out with a giggle of her own:

"Grant is taking her *for granted.*"

The two of them collapse in laughter which catches Brian's attention. He finds it heartwarming to see how well the two females in his life get on together. Excusing himself from the employees he's been speaking with he joins Lila and Beth asking *what's the joke?* and they simply nod their heads in Judith's direction. Grant is trying to monopolize her while she politely keeps drawing Andy into their conversation. Andy speaks in a loud voice, attracting attention, while giving Judith intimate looks and smiles. She's starting to look flustered.

"Lila, go be a good hostess before our guests come to blows over there."

Lila controls her chuckles and makes her way into the tension surrounding the threesome.

Judith catches herself in a yawn and, apologising for it to the two men, stands up preparing to leave. They both stand as well and Grant manages to edge Andy behind him with his shoulder. He takes Judith's hand saying:

"When I saw your car here I had Reg drop me off if that's okay...?"

"Of course I'll give you a ride," replies Judith, removing her hand and mentally shaking her head as she thinks *men are so strange.*

Stepping around Grant she says goodbye to Andy thanking him for catering to her, and saying it's been a pleasure to meet. He takes her extended hand and holds on to it for a beat too long saying:

"It's been my pleasure to meet you, Judith. I really enjoyed our conversation and hope we can continue it. I'd like to call and maybe we could get together for a coffee? but I'm still getting settled in right now."

Judith just smiles. She wants to say goodbye to Lila, and also to thank Brian and Beth for their hospitality. Turning she finds Lila at her elbow and gives a little *Oh!* of surprise that makes them both laugh. Lila takes her arm and asks what is happening with Grant. Judith explains that she is taking him home.

"Sweet."

"Oh you! just never mind. Brian and Beth thank you both so much for inviting me today. The food was delicious, I'm absolutely stuffed, and I really enjoyed being out in the nice weather, and meeting everyone."

Brian leans in to give Judith a peck on the cheek telling her she is always welcome. Judith feels a shiver – a creepy feeling as if someone is watching her – and turning discovers Andy staring intently for a moment before he grins and waves goodbye.

While they walk to the gate she turns to Lila quietly says:

"Andy mentioned he'd like to meet for a coffee but if he asks for my number please don't give it to him."

Lila squeezes her arm saying, "I would never do something like that."

"Well, you did give it to Brian, in fact you saved it in his Contacts list."

Laughing, Lila exclaims: "That's right, I did! Oh that was ages ago," and her expression sobers as she says, "So much has happened since then."

"Yes, for starters you've kept Brian all for yourself!" Judith smiles and joins Grant who is waiting for her on the driveway.

When they are seated in her car Grant leans over to give her a kiss. Judith responds with closed lips then pulls back, giving him a quick smile. Starting the car she reminds him to buckle up.

Once they get going Grant lets his head fall back and closes his eyes with a deep sigh.

"Long day for you?" asks Judith.

"Mmm, and unfortunately things are getting murkier. Tomorrow I'm seeing a family member I only just found out is actually here. I knew she existed but thought no one had seen or heard from her. Did you know Barbie had a sister, Bonnie? Although no one has, apparently, seen or heard from her for a few years she's been living in the area for some time."

"I never knew about her... Barbie really wasn't one to talk about her past much. It really is a shame you never met her because it's hard to explain the effect she had. Words don't do her justice but vibrant, alive, funny, sparkling are the closest I can come. She talked a mile-a-minute, her laugh was practically a yell, and although she wasn't pretty she attracted everyone around her. Like she was a magnet and they were all in her orbit.

I know that sounds fanciful but honestly, photos can't possibly show you her vitality or clue you in about who she was. It's just so sad that she's gone... and so hard to believe."

Grant opens his eyes to look at Judith when he hears the emotion in her voice. His concern is obvious and he want to reach out and take hold of her hand but knows she wouldn't like that while driving. Judith's hands are always in the *ten to two* position on her steering wheel. He'd told her that nowadays new drivers were being taught *nine and three* and she'd simply said *Hmmm*.

Sitting upright Grant notices they aren't heading to Judith's apartment.

"Are we going to my place?" he asks.

"Yes of course, I said I'd give you a lift home."

"Oh! I thought we'd go... no problem, my place is tidy enough for a guest."

"I'm not coming in Grant, it's already getting late, you're tired, and you've got a busy day tomorrow. There, that's three good reasons for me to just drop you off."

"I can think of one excellent reason for you to come in with me," he murmurs, leaning in as closely as the seatbelt allows.

Judith only smiles and turning into the driveway leaves her car running as she tells him *good night*.

Grant knows he shouldn't say anything but his mouth refuses to shut up and his tone is belligerent when he asks:

"So is *Andy* going to take you out for a coffee, or...?"

Judith narrows her eyes at him, the hurt confusion she'd experienced over the past several days morphing into anger, as she quietly says:

"Or what?"

"Oh, I don't know Judith what do you think? What do you think a man like that wants from you?"

"He might just enjoy my company, like me as a person, want to be around me and spend time getting to know me, but you're right – he probably just wants what you already had."

Grant grabs her hand off the steering-wheel and brings it to his lips answering quietly but with feeling:

"Have, Judith. What we had and still have."

She removes her hand from his grasp, but gently, and giving him a speculative look replies:

"Why are you only interested when you think some other man is?"

"I'm not! That's not true, Judith. Don't say that. You and I, we... we have something special. At least it's special to me and I thought you felt the same."

She tilts her head and in that movement the light from the garage door picks out the glint in her eyes, wet with unshed tears. Turning her face to look straight out the windshield, away from him, she repeats:

"Goodnight, Grant." and refuses to look at him again.

Covid-19 Updates: By May 3rd with less than 100 cases of Covid-19 the first wave has ended in Alberta. The plan is to re-open with *Stage One* on May 13th.

Chapter Twelve

Friday, May 1, 2020

Grant has been replaying last night's conversation with Judith in his mind all day. It doesn't make sense, he can't understand why she acted the way she did. Reg notices that his partner is distracted but senses Grant isn't keen to discuss his personal life. Figuring Grant will say something if and when he wants to Reg doesn't ask any questions. When they part company for the day Reg simply reminds Grant to call him if anything comes up.

Driving home Grant finally comes to a decision. He doesn't want this divide between him and Judith to grow wider so he has to get together with her to sort things out. He didn't sleep well – he hated the way they left things – and that's not good, he needs to be alert and focused in his job. They need to talk.

He can't take her out for a meal because restaurants are closed for in-person dining. He thought of offering to cook at his place, but after the cold shoulder he got he thinks she might take that the wrong way. *And she'd be right to think that,* he tells himself. He's not even sure if she'll talk to him on the phone, never mind planning a *tete-a-tete* in his bachelor pad. He chuckles to himself over that outdated phrase but Judith is a bit old-fashioned or at least not *au courant* with modern thinking. That's one of the things he likes about her. Really likes.

Feeling cowardly he taps the Message icon on his phone and sends her a text:

Grant: 2nite?

Judith: 6 my place

Grant: great *[grinning face emoji]*

Judith: *[thumbs up emoji]*

He's glad they're meeting early. This way they can have their talk, figure out something for a meal and then, well... Feeling his chin Grant decides to shave. His beard grows in heavily for such a fair-haired man and it comes in several shades darker which he thinks looks scruffy. He wants to look and feel good for Judith tonight. Thinking that, he decides he should change his clothes and if he's going to do that he might as well shower, too. He's got enough time.

He needs this busyness to occupy his mind. He doesn't want to be scripting scenarios for their talk, that never goes right and this is too important to... that makes him pause to think. This thing with him and Judith is really important to him. Judith is really important to him. He didn't think he'd been taking her for granted but maybe? Well, he'll fix all that up tonight.

Putting her phone down Judith tells Lila to call Brian and ask him to come over before six. She wants company when Grant arrives. She also wants to gauge his mood when he sees they're not alone. Judith still feels resentful about his possessive behaviour at Brian's barbeque. It makes her wonder if he'd have been quite so attentive if Andy hadn't been sitting so close flirting with her?

"Sure, I'll give him a call."

"Oh sorry, you guys don't have plans tonight, do you? I mean it is Friday night..."

"And we're in the middle of a pandemic where everything is closed. Can't go to the show, can't go to a restaurant, certainly can't go nightclubbing... oh hey, can you just imagine Brian under the strobes on a crowded dance-floor bopping along to techno-pop club music?" Lila's laugh is musical.

"No, I definitely can't!"

"That's for sure. Omigod I'm gonna have to share my mental picture with Beth. She'll pee herself thinking of her Dad in a hot room crammed with screaming, sweaty twenty-something's high on Ecstasy and puking up shooters as fast as they knock them back!"

"Ewww, gross! but you're right, there's plenty of binge-drinking going on with the younger crowd."

"Yeah, but I heard that drinking has dropped out of popularity with thirty-year-olds. Not sure if they've had enough, or if they're all smoking pot. Anyhow, Brian told me Beth was going to watch TV at a friend's place, a show on some subscription channel he doesn't stream, so we were just going to hang. I have a ton of leftovers from Mrs. P in the car that I was taking over there, and I know Brian's still got food from last night that I'll tell him to bring and we'll make it a pot luck supper. We can't stay late though, he'll want to be home when Beth gets back."

"He's a good Dad, eh?"

"You know, he really is. He's pretty much raised her all by himself and she's a great kid so yeah, he's been a good father to her."

"She is great and it's so nice to see you three getting along so well together. I mean, I've heard girls can get jealous if their fathers start dating–"

"Not Beth," laughs Lila, "She's the one playing matchmaker! Anyhow, what's the scoop for tonight?"

After a filling and varied meal the foursome are sitting in Judith's living room with coffees.

"I know you can't talk specifics about the case you're working on, Grant," says Brian sitting comfortably with his arm draped over the back of the couch, hovering near Lila's shoulders. "But this woman who was murdered left behind a family, eh? and I heard it's an extended family type of thing with a mix of blood and non-blood relatives so I can't help but feel sorry for those kids."

"Oh pffft, Grant can tell us stuff. When the legal community trots out that official line it's either to prevent a lawsuit or hide incompetence. Believe me, back in Toronto at my family get-togethers, which means lots of cops present, everything is openly discussed and opinions are given and debated. It's not natural to be all hush-hush about your work and it's probably not healthy either."

Grant chuckles at Lila's forthright comments. Taking Judith by the hand he says:

"As a matter of fact, I have discussed cases with Judith. She's a great listener with a sensible attitude and helpful insights. You've been my sounding-board a few times now, haven't you?"

Judith returns his smile, but withdraws her hand disguising the gesture by reaching for the coffee pot and offering refills before saying:

"But now Grant has Reg so I've been sidelined."

"Whose Reg?"

"My new partner. Bit of an odd situation, actually. He transferred here from the East Coast because he's really close to retirement and wanted to get settled in Alberta where his adult children live. Oh! that's an oxymoron, right?"

"I guess, but I don't know how you'd say children-that-are-adults in any other way."

"And when did you become a Grammar Expert?" laughs Lila.

"Stop interrupting Grant," teases Brian right back at her.

"Yeah, or I'll lose my train of thought. I've been suffering a bit of brain fog lately."

Grant is replying to Brian, but he glances up at Judith as if sharing something with her.

"I haven't met Reg but I'm sure he must be an improvement on Suzanne – we all met her, remember? she sent you on a wild goose chase, Brian, and her actions might have put Beth in greater danger and all because she resented Grant's friendliness towards me. Which was just professional courtesy anyways."

"Maybe to be begin with..." murmurs Lila. Judith gives her a look and Grant coughs to cover up a laugh.

"Okay anyhow, yes Reg is a great improvement. Given that I'm guesstimating him to already be at retirement age, or nearly there, I don't know how long he'll stay, but the experience he brings and his no-ego attitude is fantastic. I hope he sticks around for a good while yet. Suzanne is well, frankly, her behaviour is often inappropriate. She has a good brain and she knows the law but her brash aggressiveness is just... I don't know how to explain it but with Reg it's calming just to be around him.

But, I still rely on having you to talk to, too, Judith. And you two as well, Lila is right – there are no state secrets in this case. However, my thoughts really are too muddled and I'd kind of like to have a night off from it all. I know I've been neglecting Judith and..." he raises his voice when she tries to interrupt, "It's not just because that guy Andy was all over you at the barbeque."

"He wasn't *all over me*, Grant."

"He was trying... okay, okay. I'm dropping the subject. Instead I will say, Brian since you mentioned the kids, that one thing about this case that has stayed with me is how many have now lost a mother. Barbie Nichols was a wife, daughter, and sister, but most of all she was a mother. Even if it appeared she gave up the twins. Well, never mind appeared, she really did do that, but Moira explained that Barbie feared for their safety and her own, too. And rightly so, as it turned out because the ex-boyfriend was violent with Moira as well."

"I wonder if the older girls resent the fact that their mother raised their half-sisters?"

"Barbie was always broke. I think the twins had a better lifestyle with their grandmother. That's not to say they shouldn't have been with their mother but... sometimes you don't get to choose," put in Judith.

"So Barbie had four daughters."

"And a stepson, Gary."

"So she and Gary's father are married?"

"Yes, she had the first two girls with a boyfriend which is why she was able to leave them with her mother, she was their sole guardian – they didn't even have their father's name. It's different now, I hope, but back then? I doubt if the would have even found a lawyer willing to represent him if he had tried to get custody."

"Okay so at some point Barbie married a man who was divorced? widowed?"

"I don't know... hmm, that could be important. Thanks, Brian."

"Oooh you mean a jealous, murderous ex?"

"Uh no, Lila, I didn't mean that at all. I was just thinking that if the first Mrs. Nichols is alive maybe that's where Gary is."

"Oh that's right, he's missing. Is there a search going on?"

"A BOLO has been issued—"

"I thought that was just an American thing from cop shows on TV," interrupts Brian.

"No, we send *Be On Look Outs* too," answers Grant with a smile. He continues saying: "And there's a Missing Person post on Crime Stoppers but there are issues. First of all he's an adult, and secondly there's some dispute about when he was last seen. Plus, his father's insisting that he isn't actually missing,"

"His father's saying that?"

"He's afraid we're going to think Gary has run away because he murdered his stepmother."

"But isn't the flip-side to that the fact that one family member has been murdered and another is missing so that's cause for concern – even alarm? Believe me, I've been there and I know what an awful feeling it is when your kid is missing. Especially when... well, that's all in the past now, and it all ended well."

Grant feels a momentary shame remembering the incident with Beth. Judith's gaze is sympathetic but he isn't sure if that look is for him or for Brian.

"You've had to be both father and mother to Beth so it affects you strongly," says Lila adding: "And a missing twenty-year-old male is way different from a missing fourteen-year-old girl."

"That's true, but we are concerned about Gary, nevertheless. I'll follow up with Greg Nichols about Gary's mother."

"There's a lot of missing mothers in this case, aren't there?" said Judith. "Brenda and Glenda grew up with a missing mother who is now dead, Gary's mother is well... we don't know yet but certainly not part of his day-to-day life, and the two younger girls have lost their mother. Barbie's mother stepped up to take in the twins but then she moved them away."

"You think the case revolves around Barbie as a mother?"

"I don't know, it's just... well look at us. My mother is gone and she wasn't very present even when she was alive. Beth lost her mother when she was quite young wasn't she, Brian? Oh! I'm sorry, maybe I shouldn't mention that..."

"Not at all, Judith. I was devasted when Mandy, Amanda, died. She left such a huge hole in my life and for a long time I didn't like to talk about that, but now that I've met Lila I feel I have another chance." The two exchange smiles and Lila explains:

"Mandy died of lung cancer."

"Right, and she actually lived three months longer than the doctor's predicted. I mourned Mandy, but we knew what was happening and were able to prepare somewhat. My big fear was raising Beth who at age six needed every bit of attention I could give her and more. My mother lived nearby, she's still alive but now they're down in Florida, however at the time both she and Dad were wonderful supports to us. Family makes a difference."

"That's true. I've got sisters and they've all got families but my father's in a nursing home, not senile thank God, but very frail, and my mother passed which really left a gap."

"I didn't know that," says Judith. "I can tell you really miss her, too."

"I do. You know, when things go bad people want their mothers, they want *mommy* to comfort them and *make it all better,* but what I found was how much I miss Mom when something good happens. I mean, she was my biggest fan so any good thing in my life always gave her so much pleasure and I loved bringing her good news. She was always on my side and certain I deserved everything I ever got."

"Huh, that's true Grant, but I never thought of it before," says Lila. "When bad things happen I tend to shield my parents, not telling them because I'm hoping I can make things right and maybe they'll never have to know, but something good? I can't wait to share with them, especially Mama. And yeah, you're right about mothers being our number one cheerleaders."

"Unfortunately not all mothers, but we survive. What cliche can I think up? umm... oh yes, *we have to play the hand we're dealt.*"

"Oh Judith, I forgot. Sorry, I hope I didn't upset you." Lila looks concerned.

"Not at all, but speaking of upsets I'm not sure I've forgiven Grant for the upset he caused Brenda."

"Brenda? the good twin, right? what did I do to her?"

"You arrested Glenda! and she's not the *bad twin* she's just a girl who has difficulties with school–"

"Not just with school, she's got a bug up her butt against the police and that's entirely her own fault. She got picked up for an impaired driving charge and–"

"But she's not old enough to drink," interrupts Judith.

Lila replies saying: "That makes it worse. She doesn't have to have any particular amount of alcohol in her bloodstream, you know how it's .08..."

"Sometimes .05," puts in Brian.

"Yeah, well if the driver is underage even a sip of alcohol will result in an impaired charge."

"So do they bother to measure it? like with a breathalyzer?"

"They did, and got a blood alcohol reading of 0.02 which would mean nothing for you, Judith, but for an underage drinker behind the wheel it means an impaired driving charge."

"Why did she get stopped, was she driving erratically like all over the road or something?"

"No, nothing like that. She got caught in a spot check and her mistake was she answered honestly when the officer asked if she'd had a drink. She said *yes, one beer about an hour ago.* He was ready to let her go when he noticed she had a Class 7 licence, a learner's. Even if she wasn't underage that means a zero alcohol tolerance and automatic 30-day suspension."

"So she's penalized for her honesty?"

"No, Brian. She's penalized for breaking the law. Even if she hadn't had a drink once the officer saw the licence classification she was in trouble for driving on her own, first of all, and also for driving at night. That's two more violations including fines and the car, it was her mother's which she'd taken without permission, was impounded for a week."

"When Glenda messes up she goes all out!"

"She's also a very unpleasant girl, with a huge grievance against the world, sullen and sarcastic with a permanent scowl and a foul mouth to go with it."

"So a typical teenager then," puts in Lila.

Brian turns to her saying: "Beth's not like that."

"Exactly! Beth isn't typical, she's a sweetie," patting Brian's arm Lila adds, "Good job, Daddy." He quirks an eyebrow and smirks at that appellation which Lila quickly amends to *Dad* with a giggle.

"And I didn't arrest her–"

"But Brenda didn't know that when she arrived here in tears late at night. I was on the phone with Lila when the buzzer just rang and rang and it was poor Brenda in a panic saying you'd arrested her sister for the murder of their mother. She said she saw you take Glenda away to the police station."

"Well yes, but Glenda wasn't under arrest. She wouldn't co-operate and wasn't taking it seriously so Reg suggested a formal interview and he was right, that did the trick. Her grandmother was with her the whole time."

Grant is looking aggrieved but Judith still feels angry on behalf of both girls.

"Brenda was beside herself and I couldn't let her come in, I had to turn right around and drive her back home. She cried the whole way and was still crying in the car in their driveway when Glenda came out of the house saying you'd had to let her go."

"Oh that's just misrepresenting the facts!" Now Grant is annoyed but can't help noticing how attractive Judith is when her colour is high. She's drawn herself up with her shoulders thrown back and her chin thrust out, and he just wants to take her in his arms and kiss her. Lila and Brian are watching the argument with amused interest. As Grant advances Judith stands her ground.

"To even *think* about accusing a seventeen-year-old of matricide!"

"I did no such thing as you very well know. I can't be responsible for what you thought happened. I'm having trouble right now trying to figure out what's going on in that head of yours."

Judith narrows her eyes and thins her lips and stares long and hard at Grant. He refuses to back down and just holds her gaze with an expressionless face. As if she suddenly remembers they aren't alone Judith breaks away and apologizes to Lila and Brian for the argument adding:

"What a terrible hostess I am!"

"No, no it was my fault for bringing the subject up in the first place," says Brian.

"No, I overreacted but Judith. it's only because I don't want you to think badly of me," confesses Grant.

"I don't, Grant, really I don't."

He grins at her and gets a grudging smile in return. Beth takes hold of her and Brian's coffee cups and stands up saying they have to be on their way. Judith makes a halfhearted attempt to keep them longer while Grant is already shaking Brian's hand and giving Lila a cheek kiss goodbye. The couple are out the door in a matter of minutes leaving Grant and Judith alone to face up to their situation.

Lila awakens slowly thinking it she is far too comfortable to have to open her eyes and get up. She feels warm and cozy as she snuggles deeper into the soft blanket. Soft blanket? that does make her open her eyes. *This is Brian's couch,* she thinks, looking around the room. She's in the den, covered up by the plush fleece blanket he keeps on the loveseat and she is wrapped up in his arms. Lifting her head from his chest she meets his gaze.

"Is it good morning?" she asks. He smiles and answers *not yet.* Straightening up Lila realizes she's fallen asleep sitting in Brian's lap. Sliding over to the side she immediately finds herself missing the warmth.

"What time is it?"

"The clock just chimed so it's just a couple of minutes past eleven."

"Ha! It's your grandfather clock that probably woke me."

"I should set it to sleep mode. Then it only chimes from 7:00 in the morning I think it starts, until 10:00 or 11:00 at night."

"Did you sleep?"

"No, I was too busy enjoying myself watching you. You made a lovely bundle in my arms."

"Oh God, did I drool?"

He laughs in surprise adding:

"No, but I might have. You're beautiful, Lila."

"And you are a very sweet man who just happens to be extremely handsome yourself."

"Handsome, am I? Hmm, what about *hot*?"

"Oh very, very hot. No worries in that department, mister."

Brian pulls her in for a kiss, a long passionate kiss, and Lila feels her body respond. *No, it's too soon!* she thinks. *Arnie's funeral was only two months ago.*

But then a voice in her head reminds her that she and Arnie had separated almost ten months ago. Their marriage had ended last June, at the start of the summer. She left and Arnie let her. She moved 2,000 miles away and it was more than six months before he even came to see her – having changed nothing and seeing no reason to do so. She was prepared to divorce him, but then he died. That wasn't the reason he was dead but she kept blaming herself.

Although her thoughts are far away she continued staring into Brian's face. Yes he was very handsome – and hot – but he was also a kind, caring, and serious man. And he wanted her. He wanted to make her a permanent part of his life and give her a second chance at happiness. Marriage, a stepdaughter, a family of her own, finally, and maybe a child of her own, their own.

Lila places her hands on either side of Brian's face and leans in to kiss him back, returning his passion, deciding the time had come to stop mourning. After all, it wasn't from losing Arnie because that had happened long ago. No, she'd been mourning something she and Arnie could have had but let slip away. She had been mourning a life that might have been and it was time to start living the life she could have now.

The look Brian gives her is hopeful, but he isn't pushing, he's patiently waiting. He's giving her time to think her thoughts and come to a decision. Lila decides to choose him.

Covid-19 Updates: Attendance at indoor and outdoor wedding ceremonies is limited to 10 people including the bride, groom, officiant, witnesses, photographer, and guests. Since no food or drink or dancing is permitted there are no wedding receptions.

Chapter Thirteen

Saturday, May 2, 2020

I should be annoyed with myself for letting Grant stay the night, thinks Judith, but this morning has brought such lighthearted happiness she can't regret a thing.

Last night, after Lila and Brian left, she and Grant returned to the couch and their coffee and their conversation but... he'd suddenly pulled her to him in a crushing embrace and kissed her hard on the mouth. It was a very determined kiss, passionate and claiming, and it served to melt Judith's doubts and worries away. Next thing she knew they were in her bedroom and she was pretty sure they'd been lip-locked the whole way there.

He really is awfully good-looking, she thinks, studying his face while he sleeps. *I guess I'll just have to see how he behaves going forward.*

Grant opens his eyes, a pale blue that Judith finds very attractive, and with a smile rolls on top of her with a kiss.

"Morning, beautiful," he greets her when they finally break apart.

"I'm no beauty, Grant."

"You are to me, and I don't care what other people think. In fact, I'd be happier if I thought other men didn't find you beautiful but, beauty isn't just an arrangement of facial features, Judith, it's you."

"I would never have figured you to be the jealous type."

"Me neither, 'cause I never was before. Not until you... you're wrecking me, woman!"

"You know, when we're out I see women give you admiring looks and then they look at me as if they're trying to figure out *why her?* I mean, it's not surprising because you are a very handsome man. I was just thinking that when I watched you wake up, and I know Lila thinks you're hot. And Suzanne Mirteau certainly did..."

Grant rolls over onto his back and flings an arm over his eyes saying:

"Ugh, don't mention Suzanne when I'm feeling so relaxed and happy. She makes my skin crawl."

"I think most men would put up with a lot from her because of her looks and her sexy behaviour–"

"A lot of men are welcome to her, just not me. Now come here, I know a great way to get you to stop talking nonsense...'"

Lila is singing along with ZZ Top as she navigates her sporty Mazda into the Visitors Parking area at Judith's apartment. Her car is only a couple of years old but she racked up plenty of mileage when she drove here from Ontario. Since then she's made numerous drives around Kananaskis Country to explore the surrounding Provincial Parks. Even after switching off the engine and silencing the music she's still loudly humming the tune as she sends a text to Judith.

Lila: u free for a visit

Judith: always

Lila: good im here

Grant is in the shower but it's not like Lila doesn't know about the two of them so... Judith opens her apartment door to greet Lila just as Grant calls out:

"Judith? can I keep a razor here? I hate this scruffy look. Good thing I shaved last night before I came over, but still– oh! Lila!"

With a big grin the blonde answers:

"Hiiiiiii Grant, fancy meeting you here."

Judith just shakes her head and pushes her friend towards the living-room. Giving a pointed look to a shirtless Grant suggests he finish dressing before joining them.

"Don't bother on my account," Lila shouts out with a cheeky laugh, "I'm enjoying the scenery."

"Ha-ha," says Judith but with a smile. "You're in a good mood, what brings you by so early on a Saturday?"

"Well,I didn't think we'd have an audience but I don't care, I have to tell you, I slept with Brian last night!"

"Wait, what!? Really?"

"Yeah and omigod Judith, it was wonderful." Lila lowers her voice but the apartment is small and both women figure Grant can overhear. Judith drops her voice as well to say:

"I can't believe it, I didn't think you were planning, well I know you've been seeing a lot of each other, but with Beth around, and.. oh wow. This is so exciting... such juicy gossip!"

"I know, I certainly hadn't planned on it and neither did Brian. I mean, he told me a while ago that he wanted us to get serious but was willing to wait until I was ready. I knew we'd get together at some point I just didn't think I was ready yet, but last night it just hit me that I was ready and it was time."

"Okay, give me a minute to untangle that sentence... Okay, I figured it out and I'm so happy for you!"

They didn't realize they'd grabbed hold of each other's hands until Grant enters the room saying:

"You two look so girly, what's going on?"

Judith doesn't speak, she just looks at Lila, who answers Grant saying:

"Well, you know how you woke up here this morning? Well, I woke up at Brian's place," then sits back with a satisfied smirk.

"Oh, you mean you fell asleep on his couch watching TV?" enquires Grant with a dead-serious expression but Lila knows he's teasing so she tosses a cushion at him which he easily catches. "So you two want to have some girl-talk time, eh? Well, I can make myself useful in the kitchen."

"Coffee's in the carafe, Grant," says Judith, turning to Lila and offering a cup.

"No, not for me thanks. I'm not really staying. Brian's coming over to my place so I'm going to swing by the grocery store and then clean my home. Beth's having a friend in for a sleepover tonight so Brian doesn't have to rush back home or anything."

"Look Grant, Lila's actually blushing!"

"Yeah well... Grant go in the kitchen so we can talk without me blushing 'cause you're around."

"I can take a hint. I'll get breakfast going."

As he leaves the room Lila confides to Judith that she really doesn't care if Grant knows, she just prefers to talk to Judith alone.

"So you're getting together at your place this evening and you're cooking dinner?"

"Yeah, I haven't decided what I'll make, I'll just see what meat looks good at the store and then I'll plan my meal. Judith, Brian is so... well, he's only the second guy I've ever been with and, it's funny, but I felt kind of shy with him. I mean me and Arnie were together for twenty-odd years and I was never self-conscious or anything, but..."

"But everything was okay, right?"

"It was perfect. Really, absolutely perfect. Brian is..." she grins, "a great lover. Very um.. attentive, and considerate, and just wow."

"Oh Lila, that's so good. I'm really, really happy for you."

"I knew you would be! and this, Grant here, I'm glad you guys got over whatever that thing was."

"Well, we still haven't talked about it, but yes, our feelings for each other are as strong as ever."

Grant comes back in with a cup of coffee and announces that he's taking Judith to the McDonald's drive-thru for breakfast.

"You do realize that if you didn't take milk in your coffee you have a completely empty fridge, right?"

Judith frowns, thinking, before acknowledging that she hasn't shopped. Actually, except for Brian's barbeque, she hasn't left the apartment for a few days. Lila stands up and says she has to get going. At the front door she gives Judith a hug and her friend, always slightly uncomfortable with expressing herself, returns it while Grant smiles at them both.

"Put your shoes on hon, and we'll walk down with Lila. I'm starving."

"I need my purse."

"Don't worry, I'm buying. Let's just go, if I have to wait until you comb your hair and then decide to change your top I'll just faint from hunger."

Both women laugh at his exaggeration with Lila adding:

"Hmm, you managed to work up *quite* an appetite, Grant."

"Ha! we'll probably see Brian in the take-out line."

Lila laughs even louder and the three of them leave together.

Covid-19 Updates: Stores allowed to open for in-person shopping have strict capacity limits. Customer lining-up to get in have to follow social distancing of 6 feet. Only one family member is allowed to enter. Arrows on the floor designate one-way aisles, along with markings at the check outs that maintain appropriate spacing.

Chapter Fourteen

Saturday, May 2, 2020

Judith unpacks the containers of take-out food and sets the table with plates while Grant fetches cutlery and condiments. He's bought lots and Judith relishes every bite. Although she avoids fast food as a rule, visiting drive-thrus are going to be part of her *new normal* during the pandemic, she realizes.

Munching on their meal Grant begins by telling her:

"I've hashed this out once already with Reg, but you know some of the people involved so I think you'll have good input. I've got plenty of suspects, too many actually, and I'm looking at someone in the family."

"I'm happy to be your *sounding-board* as you called it, Grant. Plus, I do know about these people, even the ones I haven't met, from past conversations I had with Barbie.

You know, I honestly don't believe I'm a vain woman but having my hair done has always been my personal pampering treat. Just having someone else wash and brush it feels wonderful. Good hairdressers take the time to make the whole process a relaxing, enjoyable experience and Barbie wasn't good she was great. In addition to being completely open about her own life, her own feelings, and opinions, she was a great listener who never hesitated to give advice. I remember her telling me that I'd be a fool to let you slip away."

"I never met her!"

"No, but she'd seen and noticed you when you were at the trailer park interviewing Dana Lezinsky about Holly. They were friends as well as co-workers.

That reminds me, Dana told Barbie that her daughter Glenda had been hanging around the trailer park. There was that bad element, well, you know all about that because of what happened there... anyhow, she thought Barbie should know. Barbie was pretty pissed off about it, too. I had an appointment with her a couple of days later and she was still mad. She said and Glenda had had a big fight where she told her daughter, and I quote, that she'd *beat her ass if she didn't stay outta that place.* Of course that was before the fire so none of them could have had anything to do with Barbie's death."

"I'm not so sure. I mean, it wasn't that long ago, and frankly if Barbie was causing trouble one of those lowlifes might have tried to shut her up. No one wants their business messed with when there's huge money to be earned, and Barbie might have been seen as a credible threat."

"I know about the money they make, I've seen *Breaking Bad* on Netflix. I realize that's just a show but–"

"But nothing, the money is unbelievable. Hmm, that's another non-family possibility to consider... gee thanks, Judith. You've done this to me before."

"Yeah, yeah that's why I'm here. What do you mean by *another* non-family possibility?"

"One option is that it could have been an attempted robbery. It doesn't look like anything was taken so maybe she interrupted the robber and he panicked? Another possibility is a botched kidnapping. $17 million is a lot of money and the Nichols have no security system in place."

"That surprises me. I would have expected the Seely's to have all the available protections in a sophisticated system considering John Seely travelled so much."

"You're right, the Seely's did have an alarm system, cameras, the works, but the Nichols household kept forgetting to switch them off. After emergency services started charging for all the trips for false alarms they cancelled the contract. So, that makes it possible that someone was going to be kidnapped that night but... well, the argument against either the robbery or the kidnapping scenarios is that Barbie Nichols was murdered in her bed while sleeping. She was hardly a threat to a thief or an abductor if she wasn't even conscious.

The only other non-family scenario, well until you brought up the drug dealers, that is, is a crazy person. Someone who learned about the lottery win, or just saw a photo of Barbie and decided she needed to die. That *could* have happened although they were extremely lucky to first of all find her house, sneak through it despite other people being home, locate Barbie's bedroom, and catch her alone *and* sleeping. The argument against is that the *modus operandi* isn't violent enough. Usually that type of killer repeatedly stabs or brutally batters their victim to death."

"Ugh, it's scary to imagine someone she might not even know having this whole evil obsession about her then stalking and murdering."

"Thank God it's a rare type of killing because it's really hard to find the perpetrator in those cases."

"Well, let's move on from thinking about that, then. Tell me about the family. First off, what's the story with Barbie's sister Bonnie?"

"Oh, let me tell you that one's a character, all right. They're only ten months apart, Bonnie being the eldest and–"

"*Irish twins,*" Judith interrupts with a nod.

"Well, yeah their mother is Irish–"

"No, it's an expression. Oh! it's probably not nice, certainly not politically correct to say that, it's just that the Irish aren't exactly renowned for birth control. I don't even think abortion is legal there yet."

"What are you talking about?"

"When babies are born within a year of each other the expression describing them is *Irish twins.*"

"Oh, I get it. No, you probably shouldn't say something like that these days. Anyhow, the two girls were extremely close growing up, did everything together, dressed alike, led a lot of people to believe they were natural twins apparently. But once puberty hit the trouble began. The girls had the same taste in men and, according to Moira, spent their teens stealing each other's boyfriends.

It didn't end until Bonnie *had to get married* and she moved out of the house. One day, about six months into her pregnancy, she discovered her husband and Barbie having intercourse. A huge fight occurred and her loving hubby hit her so hard blood started gushing and she was rushed to hospital. In the ambulance the paramedics handled an emergency premature delivery but the baby didn't make it. Bonnie recovered but was never able to have children after that."

"That's a horrible story. Barbie must have felt so guilty for her part in it."

"Yeah well, Barbie's guilt gets worse: the father of her twin daughters is that same brother-in-law who beat up her sister."

"Oh no. Oh, what a burden for everyone. So Bonnie must really have hated Barbie all these years..."

"Not to hear her tell it. She goes by Nikovics because *there were too many husbands to remember all their names.* Sounds like Bonnie jumped from bed to bed but managed to visit the altar each time, or at least a lot of times. She thinks it's eight but said she'd have to figure it out and why bother, what's the point? the men are all out of the picture now. Although I'll bet she's collecting alimony from someone.

Anyway, she was very calm when she related the story of the rift between her and Barbie, saying she's sure not having children turned out to be a blessing because what kind of mother would she have been? I'm pretty sure my mouth was just hanging open by this time. Especially if the look on Reg's face was anything to go by, and she saw our expressions."

"Detectives, what can I say? I was born to late to be a hippie but I fell for the romance of the free love culture. I'm too selfish to be a good mother or wife and too inconsiderate to care. I was never fussed about getting married, it's the men who always thought giving me their name would give them control. As for children? well... I'm not even sure I have a heart. If I ever did it got broken in the back of an ambulance and that was a long, long time ago... too long to count."

"I don't know what to say. I think it's just such a terribly tragic story and oh my... do Barbie's daughters know their history?"

"According to Moira no, they don't. By time they were old enough to start asking about their father he'd been declared dead. At that point Barbie could have safely retrieved her girls but they were happy with her mother and financially were living a better life than Barbie could provide. It wasn't until the lottery win that Barbie was determined to reunite her family or, as Moira puts it *buy her daughters' love.*"

"That is how it looks, isn't it? But I know Barbie wouldn't think she was buying them, she'd be happy to know she was sharing *with* them. Still. So how come Bonnie is in the area now? did she say?"

Grant has a real knack for storytelling. He's able to convey the various speakers' emotion so well it's like watching a play. Leaning forward he relates Bonnie Nikovic's story:

At forty-something Bonnie, with her long strawberry-blonde hair, bright blue eyes, and curvy figure, could be a real *cougar* except she doesn't play up her sexiness. Her make-up is discreet and her style of dress is modest. She does have a lively, vibrant personality – just like people say about her sister Barbie.

Bonnie's interest is in living a life that's fully engaged and active. No one's story is too long to listen to, it's never too early or too late or too far to travel somewhere for a good time, and she's never bored. Her excitement and enthusiasm make her very attractive.

Having spent a little bit of time in Europe and a lot of time travelling in the US Bonnie has decided to return home. She feels the need to reconnect with her roots and hopes to find some much-needed grounding. Aging makes her crave stability, and she sees settling in the Alberta foothills as the next step in her journey. She doesn't want to try to transform and re-make her physical self to compete with younger women, she wants to explore this phase of her life and enjoy it as a new adventure.

Bonnie talks about the *realness* of the people who live in farming communities and small towns, and how she's discovered her *true home* here. She's been hired on as a hostess in the kind of restaurant the locals attend for *special occasions* and the hours don't keep her working too late or starting too early. She's found a place to rent, has a car, and is certainly making plenty of friends if the non-stop texts and calls she gets on her phone are any indication.

She confirms when Grant asks that yes, settling things with Barbie was her plan. She believed it was time for the sisters to reunite as a loving family. Leave the past where it belongs and celebrate the here-and-now. The future? no, it's not promised and, well look what's happened.

Bonnie is comfortable as she answers their questions without hesitation or evasion. Her reasons for seeking out her estranged, but suddenly wealthy, sister might be insincere but there's no indication of that.

Barbie and Bonnie didn't actually meet but they spoke on the phone after Bonnie convinced her mother to pass on her sister's number. No, they hadn't texted so she had nothing to show about their conversations except her call history testifies to several lengthy chats. They were working towards getting back to the closeness of their childhood – at least according to Bonnie.

"Do you believe her?"

"Right now I don't have any reason to disbelieve her except, as Reg pointed out, her general flaky behaviour. We can connect the dots and surmise why aging Bonnie suddenly wants to make amends with newly rich Barbie but that answer isn't necessarily the right one. So Bonnie remains in the game but on the sidelines for now."

"Ah! even someone as unsporting as me can figure out that analogy," comments Judith.

"You're not *unsporting* you're just not a sports fan, but I haven't given up on you in that regard," Grant replies.

"In any regard?" she sounds challenging but her voice trembles slightly.

"No, Judith, not at all."

Their discussion goes on hold while they enjoy a kissing break. Grant pulls away first although his eyes linger on Judith's lips now soft and rosy.

"You're a terrible distraction, woman!" he says, pretending to be annoyed.

"Thank you," is Judith's pretend-meek response.

"So, the sister is down near the bottom of the list. I would have said the same about the stepson, Gary, except that he's gone missing, or run away, depending on who you speak to."

Grant pulls his cellphone from his pocket and, apologizing to Judith for the interruption, fires off a text message. She notices he uses his thumbs and comments on how quickly he types. He tells her his speed improved once he got plenty of practise.

"It's such a convenient way to communicate. I mean, if I phoned Reg to speak to then I might be disrupting his day, but a text is something he can deal with when he's ready. It's quick, too, because you get to skip all the polite courtesies like *How are you? Hope I'm not disturbing you?* that sort of thing. Brian asked a good question about Gary's mother and her whereabouts. If she died and Greg was a widower then it's possible Barbie raised the boy. Her and Greg's oldest daughter is eleven I think–"

"Shawna? yes, she's eleven and Sheila is eight."

"So, Gary's twenty now which means he would have been around nine when his Dad remarried. If Barbie had the raising of him from that age, and if his real mother had passed away, he'd have a much closer relationship with her then we first thought."

"The first Mrs. Nichols doesn't have to be dead, either. They could have gotten a divorce and shared custody, or he could have gotten sole custody, and their wedding didn't have to happen immediately before Shawna came along, they could have been married for a few years meaning Gary could have been much younger when Barbie came into his life."

"Yes, you're right. Well, I've asked Reg to get in touch with Greg Nichols and he'll find out what's what for sure. Now, getting back to Gary himself. He's twenty years old and sounds aimless. He doesn't have the grades for university, no interest in college, and yet he doesn't have a job."

"He'll be collecting CERB, and I bet he doesn't qualify for it either."

"I don't know much about that programme. I've had no need to look into it since I'm still working."

"I've investigated because the school might lay everyone off and tell them to collect this. The initials stand for Canada Emergency Response Benefit, administered by the tax department so the Federal Government can quickly get funds into the hands of workers who are unemployed to the lockdown. It's a real help to people, with none of the waiting and jumping through hoops you sometimes have to go through when collecting EI benefits."

"Why don't you think Gary qualifies for it?"

"First of all you have to lose income and if he was already unemployed he hasn't lost anything. That's why seniors can't collect it because their pensions haven't stopped. Secondly, you have to have made $5,000 the previous year and filed a tax return. Even if he had a part-time summer job at our $15.00 minimum hourly wage he probably wouldn't have made that much money over two months. Barbie complained that he was lazy, sleeping late every day then hanging out in his room on his computer. I remember asking if he played video games and she answered *probably, but a boy is just as likely to be watching porn.*"

"Then he won't get those payments."

"Oh he will if he applies, because everyone who applies gets it. Nobody is checking up, although Canadians have been told they're on the honour system and to keep in mind that Revenue Canada will be following up eventually. And since there are no deductions – it's $2,000 deposited monthly into your bank account – most people are going to owe income tax."

"So you or I could just apply and get $2,000 a month for how long?"

Until this Fall, I believe. It started at the beginning of April and I guess it could end sooner if all the lockdowns are lifted and everyone goes back to work right away. And yeah, you and I could go online right now and answer the two or three questions they ask and we'd get the money. I'm sure Gary would have done that."

"That is... wow. I mean it's great for people in need but how many are going to cheat the system?"

"Lots. And when they get caught I'm sure it'll be *I can't afford to pay that back* or even *I can't afford to pay this tax bill.*"

"That must be costing a huge amount of money."

"It is for sure. There are other programmes too for employers to collect a portion of wages or something. Pat and I discussed the *layoff-and-CERB* route and she, well both of us, I guess, will implement whatever package works out best for the school. We still have no idea when we'll re-open. There's also talk about going to online learning so nothing is firm yet."

"Both of you? Oh, right, as Bursar you handle all the financial stuff–"

"Grant! I never told you, no I guess we haven't had a chance to sit down and talk until now, but Pat wants to retire and she's putting my name forward as her replacement."

"You as Principal? that's great news! Congratulations, Judith. Oooh, I'm going to have to call you Ma'am."

Judith laughs saying: "I'm not the Queen! and nothing's definite but we'll talk about that later, let's continue discussing this family of suspects."

"Okay well, again at the bottom of the list – despite you jumping to conclusions and getting all mad at me–"

"Hey, I'm not the only one who's been overreacting lately..."

"Not my fault, I never knew I'm the jealous type. Anyhow, at the bottom of the list is the twin daughters. I can't rule them out entirely because both means and opportunity are perfect fits. An unplanned murder, weapon grabbed on impulse, both girls at home for some part of the evening."

"But what about motive? There's no motive."

"As I'm sure you're aware from all the TV shows and books you read police don't concern themselves with motive. We simply establish the facts: who, what, when, where; then present whatever evidence we've gathered to the Crown Prosecutor. It's the defence and the prosecution who have to worry about motive because motives aren't facts.

Sure, if someone's heavily in debt and they knew they'd inherit a lot of money if so-and-so died then we can *surmise* a motive for them but it's only supposition. That being said an apparently motiveless crime is going to be a hard sell to any jury so sure, we give it *some* consideration."

"You've shown that either of the twins, or even working together, could have committed the crime but since the crime in question is the murder of their mother I sure can't get my head around that. Even I never wanted to kill my mother although..."

"Although what? you can tell me, Judith. You can tell me anything."

"No, it's too horrible. I mean, I'm sure you've figured out what I'm going to say so let's just leave it at that, okay? No need to air all the dirty laundry."

She hates that her voice is shaking as though tears aren't far off. Grant senses this because he doesn't enfold her in his arms – a surefire way to force her pent-up feelings to burst free – but leans in closer and rests his palm on her hand. Her hand is cold and he presses down gently, transferring his warmth to her.

"Judith, please talk to me."

"Well... when I was going through all the angsty emotional rollercoaster of teenagehood there were a few times that I wished she'd just hurry up and drink herself to death. I mean, I always knew that was going to happen someday, as it did, and I got impatient and frustrated at being held back, trapped, by her neediness. At that age everything is *so unfair*. But now, looking back, I feel, well, guilty."

"I don't have to tell you that you shouldn't, you already know that, but I can understand the guilt feelings that mix and mingle in your head after a death occurs. Really, I do. That's another conversation we'll have later, okay?"

"So long as you don't think I'm some horrible freaky person then yes, it's okay."

"Wellll, I didn't say you weren't freaky..."

Judith punches his upper arm and laughs loudly at his remark.

"Anyhow, when it comes to teenage girls I'm deferring to you since you work with plenty of them every day so you're my *resident expert*."

"Plus, I was one myself once upon a time."

"Exactly! So what could a mother do to enrage her daughter to the extent she kills her?"

"Well... that does take some thinking about."

Judith blows out her breath in a gust, her eyes unfocussed as she considers. Grant doesn't rush or interrupt her contemplation.

"Smothering with a pillow is, probably, impulsive but not in the same way as grabbing up a sharp knife off the kitchen counter and stabbing is impulsive."

"Yes, that's very true. The pillow killer had to time it just right, waiting until Barbie was in bed and sleeping, or at least dozing, before creeping in silently, and moving into position quickly. The kitchen knife killer could just as easily have grabbed a meat-pounder or a rolling pin or a glass bowl and struck out with any of those objects, meaning to hurt and harm but not necessarily kill. There was no ambiguity in the pillow killer's intention. Although they may have regretted the act soon afterwards."

"Okay, so having figured out that I'd say the girl had to have a fairly long-standing resentment that just kept building. She would see her mother as an obstacle blocking her from achieving... something. Or, if the girl was fearful for her life but too frightened of her mother to challenge her, then she might believe this to be her only solution."

"So possibly resentful, thwarted, and angry which pretty much describes all teenage girls at some point during any given week, or desperate, deeply unhappy, and scared. Neither of the Nikovics twins fits well into either category. Glenda's sullen grumpiness isn't enough, and Brenda is emotional but very open with it.

"I agree with your assessment."

"Good to know. The remaining children, the younger daughters, are simply too young. I know children can kill but neither of those two are strong enough to smother a grown woman, not even if they acted together."

"But, unfortunately, the bickering and even fighting that's been going on in that home over the lottery win, everything from how to spend the money to pulling all the family together under one roof, will have affected the girls. If they're acting up, and I seem to recall that Shawna is quite a dramatic young lady, then they might be saying things that put thoughts into somebody else's head. Children are always upset when there's tension between their parents."

"Meaning they might unwittingly be the catalysts that made someone react?"

"Yes, but I think that's a remote possibility."

"Let's hope so, because next up is their grandmother Moira. Let me tell you about my interview with her."

"Okay but let's take a break. I really enjoyed those french fries and my cheeseburger, but I ate too much and now I need a nap. Ever since I stopped going to work I've developed a really bad habit of daytime napping, every day around this time."

"That sounds like a really great idea!"

Judith is yawning, she really does want to sleep for a bit, but looking at the smile on Grant's face she suspects nap time will be delayed for a bit... and that's okay.

Covid-19 Updates: If ordered to self-isolate you must stay indoors. If you share a bathroom or bedroom wear a mask, open a window, wash your hands often, and disinfect all surfaces.

Chapter Fifteen

Saturday, May 2, 2020

Having woken from their nap neither Grant nor Judith is in a rush to get out of the cozy bed.

"I meant to tell you, Judith, this bed really comfortable to sleep on."

"Thanks, I haven't had it long. It's one of those mattresses that come in a box and I just unrolled it and put it on top of my old box-spring. It's got that memory foam plus two layers of some other stuff. I'm glad you like it, I think it was a great buy."

"Well, it's certainly comfortable enough to stay in while we talk."

Judith gets up, pulling the duvet half off the bed with her to cover up. She grabs Grant's shirt off the floor and slipping into it says she'll grab them each a cold bottled water. When she returns Grant casts a critical eye over her saying:

"That shirt looks better on you than on me."

Judith smiles at the compliment, commenting: "Well, you are the fashion police, Grant. Always perfectly turned out to suit the occasion."

She gets back under the cover but keeps the shirt on. Grant frowns, saying:

"It will get all wrinkled—"

But Judith interrupts to assure him she does own an iron and ironing board.

"Also, why are we drinking bottled water? Isn't your school into all the environmental sh-stuff?"

"I'll let you in on my little secret. The water is in a bottle but it came out of my tap. Maybe you didn't notice but I have one of those purifying filters on the faucet so I just refill my empty water bottles and keep them in the fridge."

"Hmm, I don't know if you're clever or cunning…"

"Why not both? Now continue telling me about your suspects. I love how you turn the interviews into stories, so go ahead."

Moira is a study in contrasts. Here in Edgemont she is a grandmother and mother but at home in Toronto she's a successful businesswoman running a large Media and Communications company with a dozen permanent employees plus numerous freelancers. As well as acting the role of *mother* to the twins. She's more comfortable in her big city life than here in suburbia.

Working with creative professionals might account for the touches of flamboyance in her own appearance. She's let her dark red hair grow out while the gray is coming in so it's like half her head is covered with a scarf. She wears dark eye make-up, her eyebrows are tattooed on, and her skin owes its youthfulness to *Botox* injections.

She's a chain-smoker who wears the smells of nicotine and tobacco the way some women do with a cloud of perfume. Waving the ever-present cigarette draws attention to her hands with their professionally manicured nails worn long and fancifully decorated. The backs of her hands show her age. She dresses her slim figure in shirt/sweater/legging ensembles in bright colours but at work prefers Chanel-style fashions from the Sixties.

This trip back to Alberta is not a welcome homecoming for her. Barbie wanted her daughters to come live with her and Moira came along to settle them in – or fight for their choice if they prefer living in Toronto. She's had the raising of the girls since they were infants, but she's giving them options.

Barbie is her daughter so it's not an either/or choice, they'll all still be in touch no matter what. Their curiosity about their mother and her family, the novelty of a new place, and the possibilities of a wealthy life are hugely attractive. But as teenagers what they want now might easily change in six months time. Part of her will be hurt if the twins want to stay here but Moira decided to keep that a well-hidden secret. Barbie knew though, and in their frequent arguments kept pushing at her mother, trying to get her to admit it.

Barbie's disappointment in her mother for not jumping at the chance to give up her current life was well-known to the whole family. Barbie longed for gratitude but only got resentment. It seemed just about everybody was envious of her win.

"If she was telling you the truth Barbie's mother really had no good reason to kill her daughter. Obviously she'd resent Barbie bringing this disruption into their lives and breaking up the close relationship she has with her granddaughters but it sounds like she acknowledged and accepted that the girls would, naturally, want to explore this option and she wants the girls to be happy."

"That's true, but I got the distinct impression that Barbie wasn't willing to let her mother go back to Toronto. She probably suspected that having an out, a place to escape to, would make it harder to keep the girls where she wanted them. A bit like the children of divorced parents playing one off each other to get their own way. So long as her mother was here the girls would have to stay here. Moira may have resigned herself to returning to Toronto on her own but she certainly did plan to return, that's where her life is, and that's what was causing conflict."

"Once when we were chatting – poor Barbie must have had a real struggle with me and my lack of small talk – she asked if my parents lived near. When I said no, I'd been orphaned in my teens, she said her Dad was dead and she'd never got on with her mother. She mentioned that quite casually and I remember being envious at how easy she was about it. I always got all bristly if questioned about of my mother."

"That's because your mother put the burden of her secret on your young shoulders. I never met her but I wouldn't like her just because of what she put you through. There must have been times when it was really stressful for you to answer questions, not understanding the nuances and minefields of adult conversation."

"It was exactly like that!" Judith said, marvelling at his understanding. "Although I couldn't have put it into those words then. But yes, there were a few women who used to poke their noses into our business, asking questions about how my mother was, what she was doing? where was she today? and I always ran in the opposite direction if I saw them coming because I just dreaded talking to them. Looking back now I realize they were concerned, and rightly so, but at the time I just thought they were nosy busybodies and I was afraid of them.

Grant, all of these mother-daughter relationships are getting entangled. There's Barbie and Moira, Bonnie and Moira, Glenda and Brenda with both Moira and Barbie... do the twins know Bonnie?"

"Yes, the girls knew of her, Bonnie was still in touch with Moira off-and-on over the years, but I'm not sure if they ever met. No one has said."

"Maybe her feelings towards them are tainted by the fact they're the result of her husband's cheating? I realize that's not the girls' fault but.."

"Could be, but I think it's more likely that Bonnie is too self-absorbed to bother with anyone unless they're in her immediate field of vision."

"You really didn't like her, eh?"

"No actually, there's not enough to her to like or dislike. When you're sitting in front of her she's animated and bubbly and just wide-eyed with interest but at the slightest distraction, a text, an ambulance siren, anything, her attention snaps away and you're left wondering how she fooled you into thinking she was paying any attention in the first place."

"Oh that's weird. I'd like to meet her sometime and see for myself what she's like. Maybe she'll come to a school event to cheer on Brenda."

"She'd probably be thrilled to do that... just as soon as someone pointed out who Brenda is."

"Okay, moving on. Where does Moira fit in your list of suspects?"

"I think she's a likely candidate. Means and opportunity are the same as her granddaughters so those are covered, and I think she has enough passion to fight for those girls, and for herself. If she saw Barbie as an insurmountable problem well... I think she'd want and be able to deal with her."

"But her own daughter..."

"Who has basically been a stranger ever since she grew up and used her mother to raise her own children. Now she wants to take everything away and in return is offering a place at the family table."

"A 17-million dollar table."

"Except Moira Nikovics owns her own home in Toronto, has a thriving business, large circle of friends, and a variety of interest. Why would she want to retire from that life and move to a place where not driving means you can't get around?"

"A compelling argument, sir. Leave her near the top of the list."

"The only other one on the list left is Greg Nichols. I find him odd, or rather his behaviour is what I find odd. He told me himself that he resents Barbie winning that money because everything changed, she changed."

"I expect that's normal, don't you think so?"

"Yeah, but like most people who buy lottery tickets I've never really given much thought to what I'd actually do if I won, have you?"

"I don't buy lottery tickets."

"Of course you don't," he gives her a quick kiss on the nose to show he isn't criticizing.

"But you're right, because when they interview the winners they're very vague about what they'd like to do. They just say stuff like *quit my job, pay off the mortgage, do some travelling.*"

"I'm sure the actual claiming of the prize takes some time and then they'll be getting advice from their bank, a lawyer, maybe they'll hire a money manager of sorts... and of course the begging letters and calls and visits from strangers and friends and family will have started and, no doubt, overwhelmed everybody."

"It could be a very stressful time even while they're happy – ecstatic – about their good fortune. I can see that it would be a huge adjustment. And maybe even more so for a man to adjust to his wife having all that money. No matter how open-handed and generous Barbie is he'd still be wishing he was the winner."

"I'm not so sure that she was open-handed with her *largesse*. He complained that she laughed at him for wanting to get a sale price at the hardware store but then refused to settle allowances on the kids. He didn't mind that she wouldn't give money to her daughters, but he felt Gary should have been treated better."

"If Glenda was caught hanging out with the dodgy element at the trailer park I'm not surprised Barbie wouldn't give her money. I mean, drugs – right? but Brenda's a good, responsible girl. Oh, I guess she couldn't very well treat one but not the other. Yeah, and she's certainly not going to hand over money to her stepson if she's not giving it to her own girls. But unless someone had a pressing need I'm sure they could have worked it all out satisfactorily given time. I mean, it all comes down to the fact that it's Barbie's money to do what she wants, and Barbie was the type to want everyone to be happy."

"Absolutely true, but that doesn't really make it any easier, does it?"

"Right, but Greg Nichols is not going to murder his wife because she won't give his son spending money. I mean, in the overall plans for their future—"

"But that's the problem. Sorry to interrupt hon, but Greg does think small. He's not looking at the next ten years, not even next year. Not beyond thinking about going on a vacation and for him the ideal would probably be a cabin by the lake with a speedboat, or a camper and a couple of dirt-bikes or quads. Planning down the road? probably just some vague idea about paying for university if anyone wants to go. So, no he's still top of my list of suspects but I haven't made up my mind or anything. We're still methodically checking alibis and bank accounts and phone records."

"And you might have a new line of enquiry when Reg finds out what happened with Gary's mother, Greg's first wife. Let's hope she's not dead from an unsolved homicide."

"Judith! don't even think about stuff like that, can you imagine?"

Catching sight of her mischievous smile he pulled her onto his lap for a cuddle growling sexy threats in her ear while her grin turned into a squeal and a chuckle.

Covid-19 Updates: No pet adoptions from the Calgary Humane Society until further notice. Animals are being looked after by shelter workers, while volunteers have been sent home.

Chapter Sixteen

Sunday, May 3, 2020

The aroma of coffee in a mug placed on her bedside table rouses Judith. "A lovely, lazy Sunday morning," she says with a stretch and a smile for Grant. He's moved back to stand in the doorway, sipping at his own coffee and telling her getting any closer will tempt him back into bed and somebody needs to think about breakfast.

"Yesterday you acted like I have no food but actually there's plenty for breakfast. There's milk and there's cereal, there's bread and buns in the freezer along with peanut butter and jam and marmalade in the pantry. I can feed you, you know."

"What kind of cereal?"

"Chocolatey kiddie stuff or tasteless-but-healthy organic stuff, take your pick."

"I pick you, Ms. Taylor, breakfast can wait."

"Don't jump on the bed 'til I put my coffee down!" she exclaims then shrieks and giggles as Grant starts tickling her. "Let me drink my coffee in peace, you brute."

He stretches out on his back, arms behind his head, and watches her retrieve her coffee.

"I could just lie here and watch you all day," he says.

"You've been doing that for two days now."

"No, I haven't... oh wait a minute, you're right! I've been here since Friday night, dammit Judith I don't know why I'm paying rent when..."

he pauses and for a long moment they just look at one another. Then he stands saying:

"Have your shower, get dressed, I'll get the cereal and fixings on the table and then you and I need to have a talk, or rather there's something I need to tell you."

Judith gives Grant a curious look but doesn't ask questions as she chooses her clothes for the day and heads to the bathroom.

Grant watches her, enjoying the view, then catches sight of his unshaven face in the mirror and grimaces. While some men seem to rock the heavy stubble beard Grant despises that look on himself, feeling grubby and scratchy. And since his chin hair grows in dark it makes his head hair look dyed.

He'd been teased mercilessly as a boy over his platinum locks and always wore a buzz cut. It was his high-school girlfriend, Jenny Wong, who persuaded him to let it grow out. It's Jenny he needs to speak to Judith about. He's not sure why, but he needs to do this now. The timing is right. Grants feels a great pressure in his chest that's making it difficult to take a deep breath. *Is this anxiety? or a panic attack?* he wonders.

He sets the table and lays out the cereal choices. and a couple of blackened bananas that turn out surprisingly well once he's peeled them. He knows Judith likes to add fruit to her cereal: banana, grapes, or berries in season and apples or raisins in the wintertime. He smiles at her fresh-faced appearance when she sits down at the table a few minutes later. Wearing minimal make-up and having a no-fuss haircut means she's always able to get ready quickly.

"Mmm, this looks delicious and I'm hungry," she announces, pulling her chair up close. She chooses the kiddie cereal and slices the banana into it before looking up at Grant and saying: "Oh! let me look a shaggy face for a moment, I'm not sure what I think."

"I know it looks awful, so unkempt and messy–"

Judith leans forward, stretching her hand out to rub against his hairy skin, commenting:

"It feels a bit softer than yesterday."

"Well it's grown a little bit longer. You know I can't believe some men, actually a lot of men, choose this style. I just want to scratch all the time! and when my fingers do brush against this I hate it."

"In that case, yes you may store a razor in my spinster's bathroom."

"You're not longer a spinster, Judith," Grant smiles at her. Her cheeks colour up as she replies:

"I'm not longer a virgin, Grant, but I am still a spinster. Just as you're a bachelor."

"Huh! the only time you hear that word is when someone's talking about that TV show."

"I know what you mean but I haven't seen it. I don't care for reality TV, even though I'm sure it's scripted, it just doesn't appeal."

"Something else we have in common then."

"If you'd like, how about taking a walk while we have our talk? It looks like a nice day out and it will be good to feel the sun on our faces."

Grant thinks for a moment before agreeing adding that what he has to say is going to be difficult so he prefers privacy and could they just wander in that local playing field rather than following the popular biking/walking paths?

"The story I'm going to tell you is from my past but I realize it's shadowing my present, and our future, so I need to get it out in the open." The expression on Grant's face belies the confidence of the words and listening closely Judith can detect a slight tremor to his voice. Whatever Grant has to say it's obviously something he feels deeply. At Judith's apprehensive look he is quick to lift her hand to his lips and plant a reassuring kiss on her knuckles, telling her she has nothing to worry about.

By mutual consent nothing more is said until they've tidied away their breakfast things, slipped on light jackets, and locked up the apartment. A solitary dog walker steps off the sidewalk onto the boulevard to maintain the 6-foot social distancing rule as they approach. Judith and Grant nod their appreciation of his gesture. Less than five minutes later they are walking the perimeter of an empty soccer and softball field.

Although they'd been hand-in-hand Grant now pulls away a bit and shoves his hands in the pockets of his jacket. Looking down at his feet he begins by saying:

"Ever since I can remember I've been called *good-looking, handsome, movie star, heartbreaker*... all the flattery that women bestow on little boys. I grew up hearing that and it continued when I reached puberty because I didn't suffer with acne or braces or gawkiness from growth spurts. I had girls crushing on me even while the boys all made fun of my *peroxide blond* hair and called me Ken Doll."

Judith tilted her head to study him and encouraging him to go on said:

"Yeah, I can see that. Were you bullied?"

"No, as I said I skipped the scrawny stage so I was big enough to avoid getting picked on. But I had absolutely zero self-confidence. I was only an average student, same with sports, and I didn't have any special musical talent, or chess skills, or anything like that. All I had going for me was my looks so naturally I figured anyone who showed an interest only wanted me as *eye-candy*."

"Wow, I've never thought of that happening to guys. Give me a moment to consider this... yeah, wow. As you know I didn't have any close friends growing up but of course I would hear the others girls talking and complaining about how they got treated because of their looks. They'd say stuff like *they think I'm stupid because I'm pretty* or even worse, *just because my body developed quickly doesn't make me easy* which were attitudes they'd encountered.

But for men... I guess it's the same with movie stars, with people falling in love with your looks even though they don't know the first thing about you."

"That's how it feels. Like I don't even have to open my mouth, they already figure they know everything about me. So anyhow, I didn't get a chance to pursue girls because they chased me. Girls would phone me and ask for a date, I wasn't interested and I didn't like it. Until Jenny came along.

Jenny, Jian Wong, was my first and only girlfriend starting from the end of Grade 8 until she went to University. She was smart enough to act like a buddy and when we did kiss for the first time our lips and eyes were tightly closed! Being around her constantly became the norm and halfway through high-school I realized that Jenny had claimed me as her boyfriend and kept the other girls at bay. But I'd never actually *chosen her* to be my girlfriend.

If this was a movie-of-the-week at this point I'd have sneaked out on a date, got caught, broken up before an emotional reuniting when I came to my senses. Nothing like that happened, in fact, nothing happened at all, we just went on as we had been.

As you might have realized from her name Jenny was Chinese, but born in Canada. Her parents had come from Hong Kong years before. They spoke English well, and both seemed to accept me. Partly because I never tried to go out with Jenny on weeknights, which was a thing they frowned on. They had a very full regime for her of studying, piano and violin lessons, swimming and ice-skating, and Chinese language classes. On Friday or Saturday nights we would go to a show, or a school dance, or stay home and watch Hockey Night in Canada. And, of course, we spent lots of time just talking.

Things continued without really progressing until our senior year of high-school when we had to start applying for University and that's when it all fell apart between us. I had no interest in continuing with higher education, I had known for years that I wanted to be a policeman. Jenny argued that the job was beneath me and I explained that it wasn't a job to me but a calling. I remember being confused because I'd always said I was going to become a cop. I felt a bit hurt when she dismissed the idea saying it was a boy's dream and I was a man now."

"Since you didn't marry Jenny and you did become a policeman that means you two broke up."

"Mmm, sort of."

Judith bumps him with her shoulder, She has a wry look on her face when she says: "You're going to have explain that a bit better, Grant."

He smiles in return but his facial muscles are tight. He'd told her it was going to be a difficult conversation and now that he was getting to the crux of the matter his concern was obvious.

"Judith, I.. um.. okay I'm going to jump ahead a bit and then I'll come back and explain."

Wearing a serious expression herself Judith stops and pulls one of Grant's hands out of his pocket and wraps it in both of hers. She doesn't say anything, she's already connected with him and now waits patiently.

"Right, here goes. Jenny went to UBC, that was the only university carrying all of the courses she needed for the degree she wanted, and before the first semester was over she killed herself. Drug overdose, prescription drugs not recreational. She never touched anything illegal."

Judith is thinking she should probably be giving Grant a hug but it feels awkward, she's not spontaneous with affection. Instead she squeezes his hand tighter and stares into his eyes, willing him to go on.

"I didn't realize that Jenny had made plans for both of us to move to BC for school. Vancouver is really, really expensive but she'd been counting on us living together and pooling our student loans with her parents subsidizing the rest. Did I mention they have a lot of money? They're really well off and Jenny is, was, their only child."

Grant pauses for a moment while a spasm of pain flashes across his face. It was evident to Judith that he truly had cared about Jenny and about her parents, too.

"Even though I told her, over and over again, that I wasn't going she just didn't take me seriously. She got my high-school transcript, submitted my application, and applied for funding. When she went to get the airline tickets, about a week before it was time for her to go, I had to stop her. I was sure I could get through to her parents, even if I wasn't getting through to Jenny, and I had to try.

See, I don't know if this is still the case but back then when it came to cancelling or refunding airline tickets it was the person whose name was *on* the ticket, not the person who paid, who got the money. There was no way I could let Jenny buy a ticket in my name, it would have turned an awkward situation ugly. Well, I guess that was always going to happen.

So, I went to her house and she wasn't home, she'd run out to the pharmacy, so I was going to wait but then I thought no, I need to talk to her parents. And I did. I told them that under no circumstance was I going to university, and certainly not UBC. They were so shocked, they thought Jenny and I had just had a fight or something, so it was really hard, but I had to explain to them that I had never planned on going. Worst of all, I had to tell them that Jenny had known this for a year. They were completely bewildered and Mrs. Wong was crying and Mr. Wong was angry, but he couldn't figure out who he should be angry with. Then Jenny walked through the door.

I can still see her, clear as day, wearing her faded denim jacket and brown cords, brown loafers, the typical collegiate look except instead of books she held a white paper bag from Shoppers Drug Mart. She looked from one of us to the other asking *what's wrong?* and when her father repeated what I'd said and demanded an explanation she.. she just waved her hand as if she could swat away my words. And while I was standing right there she told them *He doesn't mean it, and even if he doesn't come out now he'll be there, with me, before the end of the month. You'll see us when you come visit us for Thanksgiving."*

"Oh no, oh that's... she was–"

"Delusional, yeah. The prescription was for antidepressants. Her doctor had written her a large prescription, well a large number of refills, to last her until she could get on a doctor's list in Vancouver. He had no hesitation to do so because Jenny was always a responsible girl.

After she flew out she phoned me a lot and it's a relief to me now to be able to say I never avoided her or lied to her. It didn't matter though, she just blithely went on and on about what she'd been doing and how much she'll enjoy showing me around when I get there. I would try to tell her about my training with the police but she wasn't interested. She treated it like it was my little hobby.

So there you have it. Even without ever making a committment I managed to break one, and break the girl's heart and mind at the same time, *and* drive her to suicide. I can only imagine how you feel about me now."

Judith has started walking again, there are lots of thoughts, feelings, and unfamiliar emotions that she needs to unpack. Some of the things she will need to talk over with Lila to try and gain some insights and get some guidance. Meanwhile, Grant's longer strides overtake and pass her so she jogs a bit to catch hold of his arm to slow him down.

"So our growing closer has made the threat of committment loom large and that scares you. Okay, Grant, I don't have the words right now but I will, later, when I process all this but for this moment in time I need you to stop," after a couple more steps he complies. Judith takes his face in her hands and stepping on her tiptoes finds his mouth to let a hard kiss convey what she feels. He doesn't respond at first but she won't let go and soon they're tightly wrapped in each other's arms, comforting with a warm embrace.

"You must see me differently–" he begins but she interrupts saying:

"I do, of course I do, and what I see makes me love you even more. I know we haven't used *the L word* yet Grant but I don't care. I love you, and I hope you love me too, but if you don't that doesn't change how I feel. I feel closer to you than ever and I want you more than ever."

When they finally pull back and stare into each other's eyes she sees his are shiny with unshed tears while her cheeks are wet from her steady stream. She swipes her hand under each eye, flicking tears away, before sniffing and declaring *this is all way too emotional and now it's her turn to talk.*

Grant tells her to *go ahead* but his look is wary.

"Okay I told you a bit of this, about Pat retiring and proposing me for her job, but we didn't discuss how I feel and what I should do and what this means and, well, let's talk about me for a bit."

Laughing, Grant gives her a loud smacking kiss on the mouth and agrees:

"Yes, thank God, Judith, let's talk about you."

Covid-19 Updates: No decision has been made whether or not schools will re-open for the rest of this semester, about two month's worth of classes. The public health authority will advise the Premier.

Chapter Seventeen

Monday, May 4, 2020

Judith surprised herself by falling asleep quickly and dreamlessly last night. After Grant's revelation she'd expected to toss and turn with her thoughts until the wee hours. Grant had gone back to his own apartment so she had plenty of+ opportunity to think, and she had plenty to think about.

She badly wanted to talk to Lila but she wasn't ready to share Grant's past just yet.

This morning, Judith wakes feeling calm and refreshed. As she goes through her morning routine of shower, toe-touches, making the bed, drinking hot water with lemon, her mind re-caps the conclusions she came to last night. Nothing has changed, what she'd figured out then still feels right.

Although Grant and Jenny were a couple for years they couldn't have been in love. Not with her being so obsessive and him being too compliant. Her lack of understanding about his goals showed she wasn't attuned to his needs. And, it sounded like Grant drifted into the relationship and then just *went with the flow*. No evidence of a strong character back then, but maybe he was neither interested nor ready for a relationship? Maybe he used Jenny, hopefully subconsciously, to keep the other girls away? choosing Jenny as the safe option.

"If any of that is true then after she died he'd have been carrying a huge burden of guilt all this time," Judith says aloud to her empty kitchen as she fixes cereal for breakfast. "Especially if his heart wasn't broken... if Jenny's death only underlined the lack of depth to his feelings for her."

Judith is immersed in her thoughts when the 4-minute timer on her phone signals the coffee is ready in her French Press. With a steady hand she presses down the plunger but her mind is still distracted. She realizes that sometime after Grant's unadventurous teens he must have been thoroughly indoctrinated into the joy of sex and she's wondering how that came about... exactly.

There's nothing hesitant, shy, or passionless about Grant's approach so did he have a wild time in his twenties? He didn't go to university but the police must have some sort of academy or training centre, and then there's the job itself with its strong manly-males vibe. Plenty of female co-workers, and even cop groupies, and if he ever worked Vice... Judith's imagination goes into overtime. Now her mind is running through shows of varying explicitness that she's watched on Netflix and HBO.

"But, that's not my business," she declares. Pausing a moment to think it over she's pleased to realize that that's truly how she feels. She repeats: "Grant's past is not my business. I'm very glad he shared what happened with Jenny and how that affected him, but there's no need for me to voice an opinion on that. And I definitely don't need or want him to share his sexual experiences with me although..." she smiles as she concludes: "I'm always happy to benefit from the expertise he's acquired."

Reg is already at his desk drinking coffee from a mug with the slogan *World's Greatest Granpa* when Grant arrives carrying a take-out order.

"You made coffee? Here? Nobody ever makes coffee."

"Well, I want to drink it so I guess I'm gonna make it."

"Good to know, and did I tell you yet that you're my favourite partner ever?"

Reg laughs pointing out that *someone's in a good mood today.*

"Yeah, and thanks for putting up with my moody nonsense on Friday," Grant replies.

"Happens. Anyhooo, I got hold of Greg Nichols last night and got the scoop on his ex."

"Ex? Divorced then, not widowed."

"Oh yeah, and the first Mrs. NIchols sounds like a real piece of work, too. But before we get into that I did promise to pass on his question: *when will his wife's body be released for the funeral?* and when I told him that's not up to us he pointed out it's almost two weeks now."

"Let me give a quick call to find out."

"Good idea, because once you hear about the first wife we'll probably be heading out right away."

Grant raises a quizzical eyebrow as he places his call. Reg finishes his coffee in a couple of big gulps then puts his mug inside the desk drawer. He stands up to put his suit jacket back on as he hears Grant winding up his call saying:

"Okay, thanks. Please just make sure somebody from your office notifies the family so they can make their arrangements. Yeah, 'bye."

"Grab your to-go cup, we might as well have this talk in the car on the way."

"On the way to...?"

"To maybe find Gary at his Mom's place? You know that trailer park on the east side?"

"All too well, I'm afraid."

"Hi Mark, it's Judith Taylor, how are you doing?"

"Judith, hello! I'm doing great, thanks. Took a long while but I'm definitely on the mend now."

Judith isn't sure if that's really true but knows some men like to play down their illnesses. "Oh I'm glad to hear that. We were all concerned about you and Pat."

"It's a funny illness, first you don't feel sick at all, then you're mildly ill, and just when you figure it's run its course wham-bam your temperature spikes and you can't breathe. Awful! Anyhow, enough about me. I know it's Pat you're phoning for, so let me get her."

"Thanks Mark, it's been good talking to you."

"You, too. Hang on..." Judith could hear the handset of the phone clatter on a hard surface. The Johnson's preferred to be called on their landline, reserving their mobile phones for emergency use. In fact, Pat had told her that Mark keeps his in the glove-box of his car where, of course, the battery is always running down.

"Judith, good timing! I'm just about to head out the door."

"Hmm, that's actually my definition of bad timing, Pat!"

"No, I can stay long enough to hear you say *Yes Pat, put my name forward for your job.*"

"Okay then, consider it said!"

"Really? That's terrific news. I'm really glad you're going for it and I'm like 99.9% sure you're going to get it."

"I like those odds," laughs Judith. "So where are you hurrying off to?"

"We're going to get some new plants to have them ready to put in at the end of the month."

"Oh are garden centres still open?"

"Well, you can get plants at Costco and probably Canadian Tire too, but this is something new. We're going to a *wholesale pop-up garden centre,* just heard about this on the weekend and there are several in town. We're going to check out the one at McMahon Stadium and I hope they've got a good selection."

"I won't keep you then, and I hope you find what you want."

"Thanks Judith, I'll give you a call this evening or tomorrow. Oh before I forget, Samira said to tell you she'll be right by your side, supporting you all the way."

"Oh that's wonderful news, Pat! I mean, we both know your secretary is the one who really gets things done..."

"Ha-ha, but probably true. She said it's good I'm retiring so I can spend more time with Mark and enjoy life to the fullest."

"And she's right, Pat. Bye for now."

"Bernice Jantz, the ex-Mrs. Nichols, walked out on her husband and toddler when she got a better offer from a flashy car salesman. It wasn't a fling, she made it clear to Greg that she wasn't coming back. In those days you had to be separated for three years to end a marriage on grounds of *irreconcilable differences*. After that time period was up the divorce went through–"

"But Nichols could have divorced her for adultery so why didn't he? thought they'd get back together maybe?"

"Maybe, but he said it's because he couldn't afford the lawyer and court costs. Or he might have just not wanted to make thing easy on her. Anyhow, I don't know if the waiting had anything to do with it or not, but the salesman never did marry her. They continued *living in sin* as I've always enjoyed calling it, for about ten years before splitting when each of them met someone else. Reading between the lines I think they'd both been looking for awhile."

"And she never took Gary back to live with her?"

"Nope, and Greg told me that every time little Gary showed up on his mother's doorstep, which happened way too often according to her, she packed him into her car and brought him straight back home. Kid didn't even get a sleepover."

"I hate to hear stuff like that. But I guess it makes it easier on us, obviously Ms. Jantz wasn't gunning for Barbie Nichols."

"Nooooo, but she did recently file a lawsuit against Greg Nichols for alimony and child support."

"Child support? she never had custody of Gary."

"True but she wanted it... at least that's her story *now*. She's got a lawyer who's ready to negotiate a settlement rather than *put everyone though all the unseemly publicity of a trial of public opinion*. People are envious of lottery winners and might be all too ready to vilify Barbie Nichols for unlawfully keeping Gary and his mother apart."

"I'm guessing the lawsuit was launched shortly after the lottery win hit the news?"

"Yup."

"But people can see right through that—"

"True, but lots of people want to think the worst. I think it's what they call a *nuisance suit* where they plaintiffs are hoping for an offer of cash to make them go away."

"Wow, she's a real peach."

"Bernie, as she'll tell you she prefers to be called, is lazy, stupid, and self-centred. Greg told me how for years his little boy would sob his heart out after yet another of his mother's rejections. When Greg and Barbie married the boy was eight, I think he said, and after the initial cold-shouldering soon settled down although he always called his stepmother *Barbie* which she seemed to prefer anyhow."

"No, she wasn't particularly maternal either. Maybe it's a type Greg Nichols goes for?"

"He's a big of an odd duck," agrees Reg.

They pull into the Edgemont Trailer Park and wander around the looping road at its 15km speed limit until arriving at a trim home. There's a recently washed Rav4 in the driveway so it looks like someone is home. Bernice Jantz has heard their car and gets the door open before they climb up the two stairs.

"Come in, both of you, I've been waiting. I can have coffee ready in a jiffy or there's beer in the fridge if you'd prefer a cold one? Hell, there's vodka in the freezer if you'd like something really frosty!" and the middle-aged hennaed redhead rattles off a machine-gun laugh.

She's wearing a bottle-green velour tracksuit that is just a shade too bright for her colouring, and more than a shade too tight for her figure. The top is unzipped low enough to show off a generous amount of sagging, freckled cleavage. Grant thinks she presents a sad picture before considering that her banter and innuendo is probably a big hit with the right kind of company, both male and female. Although her looks aren't to his taste she's certainly made an effort to achieve them with heavy eye make-up, long nails painted several colours, high-heeled slip-ons, and a lot of flashy jewellery.

When I describe her to Judith I'll say she's trashy and loud, but I bet she's the life of the party at her local bar or Legion or whatever club she and her husband attend, Grant decides. He keeps his expression friendly as he accepts her offer to *sit down and take a load off.*

"Oh I almost forgot this damn thing, here stick out your hands," she instructs before spritzing them with a large bottle of sanitizer. "Gotta follow all these new laws, right boys?" and she winks outrageously causing the men to chuckle along with her.

Both Grant and Reg decline the alcohol: *not on duty,* and the coffee: *already coffee'd out this morning, but thanks!*

"I know when Reg called, Ms. Jantz, he–"

"Oh Bernie, pleeeeez," she insists with a toothy smile that shows off a diamond, or maybe a rhinestone, stud in her incisor.

"Bernie it is, then. Well, Reg wouldn't have wanted to alarm you but we are growing concerned about Gary's continued absence."

Bernie Jantz thinks about – but just as quickly discards – making a theatrical gesture when faced with the sober and serious faces of the two big men crowded round her kitchen table. Neither one has sneaked any admiring glances at her, nor have they responded to her flirtatious moves. She figures she'd better play it straight and get rid of them before she gets bored. She'll enjoy playing up the interview to an appreciative audience later.

"Gary made a habit of running away over the years. I guess he could only take so much of Greg and that Barbie. He'd come here, well I wasn't always living here, but he'd come to me but I always had to let them take him back. Greg was his legal guardian, after all." Her deep sigh elicits no sympathy. "But at his age it's no longer *running away* so why are you looking? He's an adult, right?"

"True, but only just. He's still a teenager and he's been gone for a number of days now."

"How many days?"

"No one is quite sure when he was home last–"

"Huh! that's typical. Gary got shunted to the side now that they've got kids of their own. He was always a very jealous little boy, always clinging to me and demanding my attention, but I guess he learned to keep it hidden. Hard enough being odd man out without drawing extra attention to himself."

"Well, he's certainly slipped under everyone's radar now. And his stepmother's been murdered so we want to find him."

"Why? You don't think Gary had anything to do with that, do you?" she is avidly interested, as if discussing a character in a daytime soap opera instead of her own son.

"At this point our concern is that there's a killer on the loose. We don't know why Ms. Nichols was murdered–"

"Oh it'll have something to do with that money she won, I'm sure of it."

"You're probably right, Ms... uh, Bernie. So, just to keep our records straight–"

"Cross your i's and dot your t's, eh?" she cackles at her own wit.

"When is the last time you saw or spoke to your son?"

"Oh boy, now you're asking... let's see it would have been... hmm. What's the date today?"

"Monday, May 4," supplies Reg.

"Oh well then, not for ages. My birthday is April 1st but believe me I'm nobody's fool," she winks. "Gary always makes a big deal out of it, phoning, wanting to come around. I managed to put him off this year but he definitely would have called so I'm going to say April 1st."

Both of the policemen maintain their bland expressions as they thank her for the information and for her time. Grant isn't surprised when Bernie Jantz doesn't ask them to keep her updated on news of Gary. He's almost tempted to pretend-innocently ask *would you like us to keep you informed?* but he's been well-schooled in dealing with the public.

Later, speaking to Judith on the phone is like fresh air has swept away the lingering disgust he felt in his meeting with Bernie Janz.

"Did you call Pat?"

"Yeah, I did and she's really glad I accepted. I appreciate your support as well, you know."

"Judith, I've only known you for... five months, is it? wow, seems like more, but in that time you've changed a lot. I don't know if you used to be shy or if you were just withdrawn, an introvert, but you're so much more outgoing now, and friendlier, too."

"Most of that's down to you, Grant. You built up my confidence. Both you and Lila have been such good friends to me."

"Lila, right... I've been meaning to talk to her. Listen, I gotta go, I'll call you back, okay?"

Grant realizes he's ended their conversation abruptly and briefly worries how Judith will interpret that but he'll call her later and explain it all then.

Covid-19 Updates: No one is shaking hands in greeting or saying goodbye with a hug. Families are warned to keep small children away from grandparents and older relatives since the 75+ age groups are suffering the most fatalities.

Chapter Eighteen

Tuesday, May 5, 2020

Judith and Lila are chatting on the phone. Lila is sprawled over her couch with an espresso in hand and box of chocolates spread out on her coffee table. Judith has stepped out on her tiny balcony to get a breath of fresh air. It's hard being cooped up day in and day out. She regrets not adopting a cat while she could. Unfortunately the animal shelter is now closed for the pandemic.

Instead she's enjoying a starry sky on a clear night. Calgary is often cloudy at night, and its light pollution stretches near Edgemont.

"Grant phoned me yesterday," states Lila. "I was surprised to hear from him and really surprised when I found out why he called. I assumed it was to talk about you but it wasn't."

"You mean he's not planning a surprise party for me? I knew he was going to call you so I just naturally assumed..."

"When did you develop a sense of humour?" laughs Lila.

"When I changed. Grant commented yesterday about how I have changed even in the few months he's known me. Neither of us can believe it's only been a few months."

"Every change I've seen has been for the better, Judith."

"Aww, thanks! I told Grant that your friendship, and his too, has really made a difference. Now, what did he call you about?"

"His exact words were *how did you move past the guilt of your husband's suicide?*"

"WHAT?!"

"I know, eh? I said *Gee, Grant let's just jump right in at the deep-end.* And he apologized but said he'd told you about his high-school girlfriend killing herself and now that he's actually faced up to what happened and discussed it, now he wants to move on. His ongoing guilt over her act, despite knowing that she was being treating for depression, has always made him leery of committment. He's afraid of hurting someone else and he's afraid of getting hurt again himself, but he's more afraid of losing you."

"I would never kill myself."

"And I'm sure he knows that, knows that he isn't going to break you. You have a strong will and you're gutsy, and you have backbone. Grant wants to overcome his issues because he really wants to hang on to you."

In a quiet voice Judith asks: "Do you really think so?"

"Judith when is your birthday?"

"August 13, I'm a Leo."

"Well, lioness, I wouldn't be surprised if Grant gives you an engagement ring."

"I sure would! It's only been a few months and—"

"And Grant's old enough to know his mind, to know what he wants. He wants you, Judith."

"Is all this because of that guy Andy paying me so much attention to me?"

"That might have been the wake-up call. By the way, Andy did ask Brian for your phone number. I'd already given him a heads-up, after the barbeque, but then things improved between you and Grant so Brian didn't hesitate to tell Andy no. Plus, Brian says that although Andy has proven to be a good worker he wouldn't like to see you involved with someone like him."

"Meaning what, exactly?"

"Well, Brian said he might live in a homeless shelter but Brian thinks it's far more likely that he's in a halfway house. You know, for released prisoners? Of course he's only guessing, but Andy still doesn't let anyone pick him up or drive him to his home, it's always *drop me off downtown* so he's probably hiding something. Brian says he couldn't care less for a manual labourer but he draws the line at arranging a date with a friend of his."

"Yet he had him to his home..."

"To a backyard barbeque where Brian was present the whole time. He doesn't think Andy's a problem, but he's certain Andy has a past."

"I see. Hmm, he did tell me he was hoping to re-connect with family he has in this area."

"Yes, he's been estranged from his two daughters–"

"Omigod Lila, that's it!" Judith's excitement is evident even over the phone.

"What did I say?"

"Two daughters. Brenda and Glenda Nikovics, I'll bet you anything. I've been puzzling in my mind where I knew Andy from because he looked so familiar yet I didn't think I'd ever met him. I mentioned it to him and he said he was sure we'd never met but still... it nagged at me. Now, it makes perfect sense. I've only seen Glenda in passing but

I've spent time with Brenda, her identical twin, and yes, I'm sure they're Andy's daughters."

The two women speak practically in unison:

"But the father of the twins..."

"Was supposed to have died years ago."

"And Barbie didn't raise the girls herself because she was in hiding from her abusive ex, their father."

"Then the lottery win meant her picture was in the paper and on the evening news. That must be how he found her!"

"Do you think he killed her?"

"Oh Lila, I wouldn't have thought it of him... but what do I really know about him? I've got to tell Grant about this right away."

"This is... wow. I'm going to call Brian, too. Wait, what time is it? Oh damn, he'll be in bed already, his day begins at the crack of dawn. I'll text him. If he's asleep and Beth's home he'll have his phone turned off so it won't disturb him."

"Oh that's a good idea because even if my phone's on vibrate I get woken by the ding of incoming messages."

"Who sends you messages when you're sleeping?"

"Spammy stuff, either it's scheduled by a bot or they know it's late night and hope I'll click the links before I'm fully awake."

"Huh, I never get stuff like that. Anyhow, I am going to text Brian to warn him that he needs to be on his guard around Andy just, you know, just in case."

"I'll ask Grant what he thinks about that too."

"Okay call me as soon as you know anything."

Gary's been couch-surfing with some friends in the Trailer Park but they've gotten fed up with him still hanging around. They were okay when he arrived with a case of beer and a carton of smokes saying he needed to hide out for a couple of days, but the money he'd scrounged from the house soon ran out and so did his welcome.

His mother lives in this very same place but Gary knows better than to drop in on her. She's never had any time for him, she's never been the maternal type. It's nothing to do with him, that's just the way she is. Once he'd come to that conclusion he felt much better about things.

At least she never had any other kids so Gary knows he hasn't been dissed in favour of some younger child. No, his mom simply doesn't have a motherly drop of blood in her whole body, she isn't interested in kids or family. Not like Barbie Nichols who made such a big deal of it.

Gary acknowledges that Barbie always treated him better than his own flesh-and-blood mother but still... It was bad enough having to accept it when his two half-sisters came along but the sudden introduction of two grown stepsisters, and their grandmother, well... filling up the house with all those females was too much. Especially when he found his new *sisters* hot, and the idea of twins phew, even hotter!

At least that's what all his friends say, and say it with all the salacious drooling of healthy teenage males. But to Gary they're just one more shitty thing in his shitty life. Just when things start looking up something always comes along to bite you in the ass.

But he'll have to head back pretty soon. He's been hoping the police would have arrested somebody by now. They're always asking for help from the public meaning rats. But he can't hide out forever, what if CrimeStoppers puts up his photo and he ends up getting turned in by his so-called friends? Not that he'd blame them, they only lived in a single-wide trailer which got pretty cramped with all of them there. And if a reward was offered? Huh!

He's having to go to a lot of trouble to make a call to his father. He'd forgotten to bring his charger and none of his temporary room mates have iPhones, just Androids, which no one will let him borrow. He wanders around the trailer park trying to find someone he knows and ends up in the laundromat. This building still has a pay-phone but it only takes calling cards, not coins. Not that that matters since Gary doesn't have any change.

He finally approaches the woman who works there explaining he needs to call his Dad. She isn't willing to help until he hands over his iPhone as collateral. She makes a big deal out of cleaning it off with a *handiwipe,* then loans him her flip-phone which he has to study for a minute to figure out how to use. When he has to ask the woman for his phone back so he can get his father's number from his contacts she refuses, telling him to give her his pin so she can unlock the phone and look it up.

Gary huffs over this, he isn't happy about letting his phone out of his hand sto begin with, but then he reasons he can change his password. He doesn't like that idea though, he likes what he's got and hates change, then he thinks *maybe I don't have to...* it's not like he'll ever see this woman again.

Gary gets hold of his father and asks if he'll come pick him up. First off Greg says no but then asks his location. Feeling aggrieved and annoyed by now Gary snaps that he's at the trailer park.

"You mean you've been at your mother's place? Huh, well you can walk from there."

"Dad c'mon, I've been at my friend's place, not Mom's, and he doesn't have a car. Can't you come get me? If it's okay for me to come home, I mean."

"Why wouldn't it be? Oh! you mean because of the police? Nobody's made any accusations or anything. You're just gonna have to talk to them, that's all. Anyhow, you're a lot closer to home than I am, even walking, so I'm not coming all the way out there to get you. Come home and we'll talk things over later."

"Walk? I don't wanna..." but his father has already disconnected the call.

The woman had heard everything and now she just smirks at Gary, holding her hand out for her phone before she returns his.

"You're welcome!" she hollers after him but the sarcasm goes right over Gary's head. He's too wrapped up feeling sorry for himself to spare her any consideration.

When he gets back to his friend's trailer an impromptu party had broken out with a few cars pulled up and a bunch of people his own age sitting on lawn chairs or sprawled on the grass. Some girl hands Gary a beer which he accepts with a grin, deciding he'd go home later or maybe even wait until tomorrow.

Maybe his old man will feel bad about not coming to get him. He can't push him too far, though, because his father is going to end up with a lot of money pretty soon.

Honestly, sometimes he treats me like I'm an irresponsible child, fumes Judith after a very unsatisfactory conversation with Grant. Her news, the connection she's made, is a revelation. She's pumped up to share it but is Grant appreciative? no, of course not. He immediately dismisses any idea of collaborating, planning or plotting. *He's such a... a CHAUVINIST,* she decides.

"And I'm sure Grant's acting like this because it's Andy. Grant's got a real grudge against him just because he showed me a little attention at Brian's party. Anybody else and we'd probably still be discussing ways and means but with Andy? no way, I have to butt out because *it might be dangerous.*"

Judith's phone rings, interrupting her monologue, with a call from Lila. She's fared no better.

"Hope you got further with Grant than I did with Brian, because I got no joy from him whatsoever. Here, I'll read you what he texted back:

Brian: the professionals can handle it so let the cops do their job

What did Grant say?"

"Pretty much the same thing except with him instead of amateur versus professional it feels more like silly woman versus sensible man. Aarrgghh! I get so frustrated with that attitude."

"Tell me about it! I basically ran things with Arnie but Brian? different story altogether. Don't get me wrong, I love that I can't push him around but hey, where's the harm in a little nudging," Lila says with a laugh.

"Oh I agree. I don't want someone who can't even decide where to eat dinner, but this *laying down the law* can go too far."

"Well, law kind of is Grant's thing, right?"

"Lila," warns Judith, "I can hear you holding back a giggle! and I'm too annoyed to laugh."

"You're such a newbie at relationships! Listen, ever heard the expression *it's better to ask for forgiveness than permission*? Weeeeellll, just because the guys are telling us what to do doesn't mean we have to do it."

"Oh! you mean we could–"

"Could and should. So, let's plan!"

Covid-19 Updates: Businesses are incurring costs to meet the re-opening requirements. Reduced capacity means seating is removed or areas closed off with signs posted on doors. Plexiglass dividers are installed to separate staff from customers, 6-foot social distancing markers are placed on floors and sidewalks, and sanitizer and cleaning wipes must be provided at every entrance and cash register.

Chapter Nineteen

Wednesday, May 6, 2020

Grant is well-aware that Judith us angry with him – again – but it can't be helped. If Andy really is the father of Barbie's daughters then he is a dangerous man. Not necessarily a murderer, but that's something they have to consider.

Today is going to be all about getting factual information. Anton Czerny was officially declared deceased so they'll have to jump through hoops to get an arrest warrant because dead men can't commit crimes. The law is often blinkered. Grant is meeting with the Crown Prosecutor's office to discuss this unusual situation. He's pretty sure he'll come out of that meeting with his hands tied. First, though, he wants to bring Reg up-to-date with this new information, and then they'll go see Moira Nikovics.

"I don't think you should bring this to Moira yet."

Grant is taken aback at Reg's opposition to his plan.

"But she's the only one we know who could identify Anton Czerny."

"*Might* be able to identify him you mean. There's no guarantee. That's one of the reasons I think it's a mistake to involve her until you have more information. Another reason is the fear and worry this will cause and maybe – probably – unnecessarily, too."

"Really? you don't see this as a likely scenario?"

"No, of course not. Grant, what have you got? besides a very persuasive girlfriend, that is."

"Judith is not fanciful, nor does she dramatize herself," replies Grant stiffly.

"I didn't mean to imply she was but.. okay, let's re-cap what you've told me. A guy named Andy has returned to this area to reconnect with daughters he left behind. He bears a resemblance to the twins whose father disappeared many years ago. And...?"

"And the missing father was called Anton, and this Andy has served time and is the right age and has no money or job or home yet he's confident the girl's mother *won't be a problem*. Look, I know it's not enough to get an arrest warrant or anything but if Moira Nikovics can give us any kind of identifying information like height, build, eye colour, age, then I want to hear it and maybe we'll really luck out and she's got a photo."

"Grant, put yourself in the woman's shoes. One, her daughter has just been murdered, and two, you're asking if the man who terrorized her before blessedly dying a decade ago might still be alive and back here now looking for her granddaughters. Do you really thing that's fair?"

"Fair? Reg, how *fair* will it be if Andy *is* Anton and he's killed Barbie and is now on his way to find his girls?"

"Oh, so you've pegged him as the killer, too?"

"Are you so sure he isn't? If there's even the slightest chance then I think Moira, and Greg Nichols, and those girls deserve a heads-up."

"Even considering the emotional cost..."

"She's a strong woman, I believe she'd want to know."

Reg shakes his head but doesn't argue further.

"You're the boss."

"No, the office of the Crown Prosecutor is actually our boss at the moment. No sense both of us being alternately bored then ridiculed so I'll go get lectured and will meet you back here.

"As I said... you're the boss." Reg repeats with a snarky grin.

Gary's temporary landlord kicked him out of the trailer after a quarrel late that night. The girl he'd been flirting with had left and too many beers made him morose and argumentative. He ended up finding refuge on top of a picnic table. The air turned chilly in the early morning hours and Gary awoke dry-mouthed and miserable. He staggered away to take a whizz against a tree before stumbling back and flopping down on the table again.

He's lain there, sprawled out, all day. At 5:00 pm a resident calls the manager, Jerry Bennett, to complain. He says he's just sat down to his supper but will check things out as soon as he finished. The lady assures him it certainly wasn't worth interrupting his meal, adding that hopefully the bum will be gone before he gets there.

So it's about 5:45 when Gary is roughly shaken awake by a big man with a red face and a small, odd-looking moustache. His colouring is the result of a two-month-old burn and the pared-down facial hair is all that remains of Jerry's once-luxuriant Fu Manchu. He's determined to grow it back, though. In the meantime Gary finds the big man intimidating, not laughable, so he doesn't argue when he's told to go to his trailer or get off the property. He sits up with a groan from his uncomfortable makeshift bed on the picnic table and absently starts scratching at the mosquito bites dotted along his forearms.

He turns towards his friend's trailer before remembering their fight and instead aims for the road out. Jerry Bennett stands watching until Gary is out of sight.

The sunshine is still bright and shines hotly on the back of his neck as he trudges with his head hanging down. He's suffering from a pounding hangover headache. The walk home really isn't that far but he's in no rush to arrive. In fact, he doesn't want to see anyone at all and sure doesn't want to answer questions. He just wants to go back to sleep in his own comfortable bed. After downing a couple of bottles of water or pop.

He'll go in the kitchen door, grab what he needs from the fridge, then quietly sneak up to his room and lock the door. He's done it before.

Judith and Lila have made their plan but it doesn't start till end of the afternoon and Judith is getting antsy. She calls Lila to invite herself over so they can hang out until it's time to leave.

"Yeah sure, drop in, are you hungry?"

"Why? is your landlady cooking?"

"Mrs. P is *always* cooking or baking something and I've got a fridge full of her dishes. Come over and raid it."

"I'm on my way!"

Twenty minutes later Judith has texted her arrival and Lila is waiting for her at the back door. As soon as they walk down the stairs to Lila's basement suite Judith smells the wonderful aroma of home cooking.

"I've gone ahead to heat up a couple of platefuls. Mrs P doesn't think much of microwaves so her re-heating instructions are always for the oven which takes longer."

"I'm drooling it smells so good!"

"I am so lucky with her for my landlady. I took Brian up to meet her and she's ready to adopt him. Right in front of him she says to me *so handsome, you better watch out for the hungry girls* and he reassures her that I keep him well-fed and of course I'm turning all shades of red because I know what the two of them are really talking about. They got on soooo well."

"He does seem to be an easy-going guy but, as you've discovered, he's just as good as Grant when it comes to the macho crap."

"Oh Brian's better at it than Grant is because he's had years of being *Daddy* with all of the overprotective behaviour that involves."

Lila puts a couple of padded placemats down then brings the hot plates out of the oven. Judith helps herself to a bottled water from the fridge and asks:

"What do you want to drink?"

"I've got a water going – do you want a glass with lemon?"

"No, this is good thanks. Mmm, and this food is excellent!"

The two women eat their meal with shared enjoyment. They tease each other about their *boyfriends* and giggle over jokes and innuendo. Judith is experiencing the giddy foolishness of having a *bestie* to confide in, something she missed out on back in high-school.

Lila's kitchen doesn't include a dishwasher so she fills up the sink with hot soapy water but Judith moves her aside saying:

"You dry because I don't know where anything goes." After they get the place tidied up again Judith suggests popping upstairs to thank the old lady for the food. Lila agrees it's a good idea but wants to check first because her landlady often takes a nap around about this time.

Judith doesn't have long to wait before Lila is back and waving for her to follow.

Mrs. Piernitsky is sitting at her kitchen table drinking a glass of cranberry juice. She gestures with the glass saying:

"Terrible taste but doctor says I need it for my plumbing. Maybe too many babies, eh?"

The younger women laugh at her outrageous wink and Lila admonishes:

"Don't be naughty Mrs. P. I'm still blushing from Brian's visit and the things you said..."

"I only talked about good cooking!" she answers with a cackle. "Do you know Brian too, Judith?" She pronounces the name *Ju-deetz*.

"Yes, his daughter Beth is a student at our school. I met Brian last December. Well, that's really when Lila and I became friendly too."

"Ah, too bad for you that Lila sees him first huh? He's such a handsome boy with that lovely red hair... shows he has the passion in him."

"Don't worry about Judith, Mrs. P. We all met because of a police investigation and Judith snagged the top cop for herself!"

"Oh-ho, the two of you both have men so now you'll be settling down?"

"Well December was only a few months ago—" begins Judith but the senior waves away that objection saying:

"With my Zoso, God-rest-his-soul, I knew right away and he did too. You two girls are pretty but you can't wait too long. If you start your family too late you'll be too old to enjoy your grandchildren."

"Wow, now we're talking grandchildren."

"Mrs. P does not mess about when she wants to make a point," says Lila with one arm around the lady's shoulders to give her a squeeze.

"Well you certainly can cook a delicious meal. That's the second time Lila's fed me with your cooking and both times were mmmm, so good!"

"If your man wants Ukrainian or Hungarian food you tell me and I teach you how to make a couple of things."

"Thank you! I'd like to learn."

Lila and Judith leave soon after having scheduled a date for a cooking lesson. Mrs. Piernitsky warns Lila not to say anything to her children since she's been rationing her time with them explaining:

"Lovely grandchildren and great-grandchildren but too much germs from the little ones."

They all exchange goodbyes and the two friends head back downstairs to Lila's suite.

"Soooo... you've told your landlady about Brian but how about your parents?"

Lila screws up her face in a grimace saying she doesn't have the nerve yet.

"I mean, I've told them about him and how I spend quite a bit of time with him and Beth so maybe they've read between the lines but nobody's said anything."

"Hmm, but if you've introduced him to Mrs. Piernitsky then, well, it's obviously serious."

"You mean because I told my substitute Mom, or because I'm sleeping with him."

Judith's eyes widen at Lila's frankness then she smiles and answers: "Both!"

"To tell you the truth I can really see us making a life together. I mean I know it's super-sudden and everything but we're adults and we know what we want and, we both want the same thing: a family."

"Yes, you'd be getting a ready-made family with Beth..."

"And, hopefully, children of our own, too."

"Brian wants more kids?"

"So much so that when I told him I would make a doctor's appointment to take care of the birth control situation he asked if I would consider not doing anything preventative, just let nature take its course."

"But.. what.. what did he mean?"

"He means to get me pregnant. And Judith? I love the idea!"

"Oh, oh I see. So if you do fall pregnant that would force the committment thing between the two of you, right?"

"Pregnancy would mean us getting married, yes."

"OMIGOD! Marriage, kids, and you love him?" Judith asks the question with a little hesitation, it seems such a personal thing but Lila just grins back and answers *Yes! Oh, yes!*

Judith hugs her friend and they're both surprised at her making such an impulsive gesture. Now it's time for the two friends to begin their tailing and surveillance but once they're buckled into the car Judith brings up the subject of birth control again, asking Lila what she was planning on.

"You being a nurse, will know what's best to use."

"Especially me being a nurse in an all-girls school full of adolescents."

"Oh right, I hadn't thought about that."

"Well Acting-but-soon-to-be-permanent-Principal Taylor it's something you better think about. Oh, we could make recommending that the students get the HPV vaccination as your first point of contention with the parents and the Board."

"Lila, let's say the controversy for another day, hmm?"

"Spoilsport. Anyhow, at our age I recommend an IUD."

"Okay I've heard of that..."

"It's a small device your doctor inserts and you can forget about it for like ten years, or is it five? No, I think I read it's good for ten years now."

"Sounds creepy."

"No, it's perfect, a drug-free solution, and you won't even know it's there. Seriously, make an appointment with your doctor to get it put in. Then tell Grant he owes me big-time," laughs Lila.

Grant begins their meeting with Moira Nikovics by explaining he has no new information about Gary or about Barbie's killer. He then apologizes in advance for broaching a subject that might cause her concern, possibly upset, before asking if she'd ever had any reason to believe the girls' father was still alive.

Moira responds with a loud laugh of disbelief, saying *of course not,* and then scoffs at them for *grasping at straws.*

"That Anton was a nasty piece of work who died years ago and good riddance. Look, I know no body was ever found but as they told us at the time it was a very, very deep lake. Maybe the Rocky Mountains have their own version of a Loch Ness monster and it got him? That would make me smile, a monster devoured by a bigger monster."

"Well it was something we had to follow up. He was actually your son-in-law, right? say you don't have a photo of him by any chance, do you?" Grant's enquiry is made casually but Moira isn't fooled.

"Look just tell me what's going on? I don't have a photo but you do – you've got a mug shot, he was arrested and went to prison."

"Yeah, I'll look into that." Grant is careful not to meet Reg's enquiring look. The file Grant had requisitioned should have had a mug shot and when it didn't he immediately looked at the charges and the suspicion he had was confirmed when he saw *Resisting Arrest.* Whether or not Anton Czerny had actually resisted he was almost definitely beaten up by the arresting officers and his face was too messed up for a photo to go in the official record. Things used to be handled quite differently – wrongly – but the uniformed thugs should have been terminated by the nineties. Obviously not all were.

Reg speaks up then, surprising Grant considering how he'd disagreed earlier, saying:

"I think you better come clean with Ms. Nikovics, Grant. I realize it's only supposition but tell her what's brought us here and then she can give us her opinion."

Moira gives Grant a skeptical but interested look so taking a deep breath and cursing himself for feeling foolish he plunges right in.

"A couple of the employees at Brenda's school, the bursar and the school nurse, are friends and they heard a story that has them connecting dots and called me with a possible tip. There's a man, early to mid-forties, called Andy, working as casual day labour for construction crews. He's newly arrived in Calgary mentioning that he has daughters here who he'd like to reconnect with after many years."

"Well sure, the age is right and Anton was a hard worker, a builder, but that's quite a stretch–"

"Thing is, these women met this Andy and they insist he bears a very strong resemblance to Brenda and Glenda."

"No."

"You're probably right, but as I said–"

"No, No! NO! Oh God, no-no-no, it can't be." Moira's fear fills the room startling both men with its intensity.

"Ms. Nikovics, Moira, please–"

"If anyone could come back from Hell it would be him, he's always been a devil. Omigod the girls! We have to get out of here!"

Reg grabs the woman's hands, easily covering them with his own big hands, and speaks to her in his soothing, calming voice.

"We don't know if it's him and frankly it's really, really unlikely so don't panic. We know where this Andy will be working tomorrow so we're planning to talk to him and we'll get a photo to show you. It's probably no use me telling you not to worry about this tonight but try."

"I am really sorry to have upset you like this, Ms. Nikovics. We never want to worry people, especially since as Reg says this is a real long-shot, but what if? I believe you're a strong woman who can handle knowing what we're investigating, so I think it's important to give you a heads-up. You should be on your guard for yourself and the girls because even if there's nothing to this Andy-Anton idea there still is a killer out there."

Moira reaches into her pocket and pulls out a pack of cigarettes. Her hands shake so badly she can't hold the lighter steady so Reg helps out. After Moira inhales deeply they can see her visibly relax. It is still a full minute before she speaks and when she does it's to thank the men for their honesty.

"Anton Czerny being alive would be the worst possible thing that could happen. Barbie couldn't fight him back then, neither could I, and the thought of him anywhere near the girls is just sickening but... no point getting my stomach in knots worrying about the possibility. Still, I'll make sure the house is locked up and everyone is careful of strangers. I'll say you told me a suspicious character was reported hanging around. I don't have to explain any more than that."

Both Grant and Reg approve this plan, with Grant adding that as soon as he has more information and a photo he'll be back.

"Tomorrow, yes?"

"Yes, we'll see you sometime tomorrow."

Covid-19 Updates: Workers forced to self-isolate, or care for someone ill, can apply for the Employment Insurance benefit. If they don't qualify for EI the Federal Government will pay them up to $450 weekly for 15 weeks. The province is paying to cover the usual two-week waiting period.

Chapter Twenty

Wednesday, May 6, 2020

"Brian? Hi, it's Grant, George Grant. I got your number from Judith, do you have a few minutes to talk?"

"Sure, I just got home from work. I never knew your first name was George, I just thought it was Grant something."

"Yeah well, Grant's what I've always gone by so..."

"Learn something new every day."

"Speaking of which... has Lila said anything about your employee Andy? What's his last name, by the way?"

"I don't know his last name because he's not an employee, just casual labour I pay in cash at the end of each day. Lila did send me a text about her and Judith figuring Andy might be the long-lost father of these girls from their school, the girls whose mother was recently murdered. Anyhow, I texted back that she needs to keep her nose out of it."

"Oh thank God. The last thing those two need is any encouragement to be amateur sleuths like that young woman... you know her, it's a TV show but... nah, I can't remember her name. Anyhow, I'm glad you and I are on the same page about warning them off from getting involved. So, getting back to Andy, what's your take on the guy?"

"Good worker. Punctual, skilled, capable, strong, and he gets along okay with the rest of my crew."

"I guess I'm a bit biased about the guy..."

"Oh I'm not advocating for him, I know there's gotta be something wrong with the man. You don't get to be that age with nothing to your name unless you threw it away via a bottle or crime or any of a dozen reasons, I guess. He doesn't talk about his past except for mentioning he's estranged from his daughters who live in this area. Oh, and he said their mother wasn't a problem, she'd remarried or something."

"Or something... hmm, I wonder."

"Do you know anything about these girls' father?"

"Yeah, he's supposed to be dead but no body was ever found."

"Oh."

"Yeah, *oh* is right. The story is Barbie dumped her twin daughters on her mother soon after their birth and then disappeared to get away from their abusive father, who was also her brother-in-law. He ended up in jail for a couple of years, bar fight I think it was, and as soon as he got out he made a beeline for the mother's place where his girls were.

After that confrontation the mother, Barbie's mother, sold up everything and left Alberta, moving to Toronto. The girls' father had gotten violent with her and she had him arrested but he escaped custody and ran into Kananaskis country where he vanished, presumed drowned. This happened more than a dozen years ago. Eventually he was declared dead, and no one's ever heard from him, but... Andy's age is right and the abusive Dad was called Anton."

"Shit."

"So, you can see why I told Judith to back off and I'm glad you said the same thing to Lila."

"Yeah, geez I had this guy at my home, around my daughter, I just.."

"Brian, Andy might not be Anton. It's only supposition based on a few offhand remarks. I did talk to the girl's grandmother, she's certain she can identify Anton Czerny if it is him. At this point I can't pull him in for a line-up but there are ways... My next step is to talk to Andy but he's not obligated to answer any of my questions. I mean I can ask for his ID and do a records search which might lead me somewhere... I was hoping you had his full name and an address."

"No, as I said if he was an employee then yes, I'd have that information, and if he works for another four days I'm going to get it from him for payroll tax and WCB because he'll have moved into a casual/part-time situation but until then, sorry."

"How does he get to work, do you pick him up somewhere?"

"I get him at *Cash Corner* do you know it?"

"Yeah, I do, what time do you get him?"

"Uh, Grant, this is starting to get awkward."

"Brian, I get it. Obviously he's going to know this came from you, but he already knows we're friends and he probably knows I'm a cop—"

"I've never told anyone that."

"No and thanks, but with ex-cons you don't have to, we recognize each other. This is better than me showing up at your job-site in front of your crew, right? If there's no connection, if the guy's innocent, well I can't say *no harm done* because he might not be willing to stay working with you but I definitely need to talk to him."

"Yeah, okay, I can see that. Damn, he was a lucky find, a really good worker, you know? But that in itself means that there's something hinky about him hanging around *Cash Corner.* Anyhow I told him I'd see him about 7:10 so we could be on site by 7:30."

"I'll be in place before 7:00 then. There's no need for you to come by."

"I think I will, though."

Unknown to the two men is the fact that Judith and Lila are already executing the plan they've defiantly put in place.

"I remember that the job site is really open, a new subdivision under construction, so no cover and Brian knows your car as well as mine, Judith. When he talks about Andy he says he always picks him up and drops him off back at *Cash Corner* so that's why we're hanging out here. We can stay well back, Andy doesn't have a car of his own so he won't be travelling too quickly. Anyhow, we just want to see where he goes, just to get an idea of what he does, where he lives..."

"And we're bored to tears stuck indoors during this pandemic so..."

"Oh look, right on time, that's Brian's pick-up." The two women slump down a bit in their seats although no one's looking in their direction.

"Yup, there's Andy. Looks like they're talking about working again tomorrow."

"Okay, and there goes Brian. He'll head home, grab and shower, find out what Beth's plans are, and then give me a call."

"You better turn your ringer off, just in case he calls at a bad time."

"Really? Why do you think...oh never mind, it's always somebody's ringing phone that screws things up in the movies. I'll put it on vibrate now so I don't forget if we get busy later."

"It doesn't look like we'll be busy at all, look Andy's just standing there. How are we supposed to follow him if he won't go anywhere?"

"Judith, impatient or what? Relax."

"Yeah, yeah. I just want something to happen, you know."

"Of course I know, you want to be able to have an *I told you so* moment where you tell Grant something startling, something he hadn't known or couldn't have figured out for himself."

"So maybe it's a little childish..."

"No, it's a lot childish but 100% understandable. So, give it a chance."

"But why is he just standing there?"

"Omigod Judith! it's a bus stop, see?"

Judith screws up her face in self-disgust and her expression makes Lila laugh heartily. Lila's laugh always sets Judith off and soon the two are gasping for breath. The overreaction is due to nerves and excitement. Luckily the bus pulls up then so they begin the tedious yet anxiety-inducing process of following a city bus at rush-hour, ignoring the honking horns and rude gestures of the other drivers.

After about forty minutes the bus reaches the city limit and the remaining passengers all get off to go their separate ways. Some are met by waiting cars, and some go into the Tim Horton's. Andy stays on the road and starts walking.

"Well that sucks," says Lila. "We can't follow him in a car while he's walking, we'll look like curb-crawlers."

"What's that?"

"That's what they call the guys in cars who go trolling through red light districts checking out the working girls."

"It's hardly the same thing!"

"No, at least they're potential customers. We're just stalkers."

"No we aren't, we're... okay I guess we are. Well, so much for that idea. I wonder where he's going?"

"Home, I mean our home. This is a secondary road leads into the west-end of Edgemont."

"I wonder if we should grab a coffee? we can kill fifteen minutes or so drinking it here in the parking lot. That should give him a chance to get near where he's going, then we can drive by and pick up his trail?"

"I suppose we could.. I can always drink a cup of coffee and oh look! he's just hitched a ride from that SUV."

"Lila, I've always wanted to say *follow that car*," says Judith with delight.

"*And step on it*, am I right?"

Covid-19 Updates: To reduce the risk of the virus entering prisons no classes or group therapies or visitations are allowed. Outdoor time and activities have been curtailed or suspended because maintaining social distancing of 6 feet is impossible.

Chapter Twenty-One

Wednesday, May 6, 2020

Grant isn't unduly surprised when his call to Judith goes straight to voice-mail, just a little disappointed because he wants to update her on what actions he's taken about Andy. He wants to get back on her good side, not liking it when she's mad at him.

He decides to leave a message: "Hey sweetie, lot's to tell you about that lead you found so call me when you get this. Kisses."

At the same time Brian is puzzled at not being able to reach Lila. They don't have firm plans for tonight but he was expecting to see her. He's sure she would have called or texted if something came up unexpectedly, and hopes nothing's wrong. He worries about her being a nurse and getting exposed to the virus.

Lila has already discussed a possible job change, temporarily, that is. She told Brian that if the number of hospitalizations jumps she suspects all of the nurses working in the province will be called to front-line duties. She also said that with the school shut down she would feel obligated to go help. He hopes that doesn't happen. The lack of concrete information about the disease makes everyone nervous.

If he knew what Lila was up to right now with Judith he'd have good reason to be annoyed... and worried.

"This is the worst possible neighbourhood to try to hide," whispers Lila.

They've followed the SUV at a respectable distance until it stops at an intersection and Andy jumps out. They're forced to go through the light but manage to turn around in the lot of a corner 7-11 convenience store.

Andy is easy to spot, there's no one else around, so they drive past him with Judith exclaiming *that's Barbie Nichols' home!* and park the car a couple of houses down. Since the properties are so large they have quite a ways to walk back.

They're sneaking along the edge of the sidewalk on this dark, quiet street feeling incredibly conspicuous. They don't dare step on lawns because of motion-sensing lights or patrolling dogs. The houses are so well-concealed behind walls and shrubbery you can't even tell if anyone is home. With nothing to see or hear the atmosphere weighs down on the two women, but they remain alert.

Andy isn't on the Nichols' driveway or at their front door so he must have gone around to the side or back of the house. Judith and Lila creep as quietly as they can and follow his path. They duck down when passing windows but the rooms are dark. The last window on this side shows a light but it's muted since the drapes are drawn.

Both women hesitate to round the corner into the back of the property. It's so dark, and leaving the protective cover of the wall is scary. Judith is in the lead on the walkway and reaching back she grabs hold of Lila's hand. Her friend's answering squeeze gives her the necessary courage. With a deep breath and a silent prayer that they aren't about to come face-to-face with Andy Judith steps out.

Being hyper alert after meeting with the police Moira is on the lookout for anything out of the ordinary. She hears a scuffling down the path along the side of the house and immediately phones Grant. He tells her he's on his way but she must keep everyone inside and call 9-1-1. They'll keep her on the line until the police arrive. He calls Reg as he runs down the stairs from his apartment to get his car.

"Might be a false alarm but Moira Nikovics just called to say someone's on the property so I'm heading out there now."

"I'll call 9-1-1 and meet you the house," Reg replies and disconnects before Grant can tell him Moira has already called the emergency services.

When Greg came home that afternoon from wherever it is where he's now spending his days – a bar, from the look of him – Moira told him about Grant's visit. Greg is utterly disbelieving and because he's never known Anton Czerny he can't understand the frightened reaction of his mother-in-law. Moira makes him promise not to say anything to the girls, neither the big nor the little girls, but to make sure they stay safe inside.

Once dinner is over Moira finds herself restless, unable to settle, and goes wandering through the house checking in on everyone. Then she makes sure all the doors are locked, something she usually doesn't bother about until bedtime. Now, after phoning Grant, she goes in search of Greg. She finds him sitting with the girls watching some new-release movie on the huge projection screen TV. They are all relaxed and safely accounted for so she backs out of the room without interrupting their show and comes back to the kitchen to call 9-1-1.

The lawn spreads out before Judith and Lila, just a smooth expanse with darker shapes along the edges denoting where a lot of trees and bushes grow. Turning her head to the left Judith sees a brick patio leading to sliding doors, the room behind them dark, and then views of lit windows on the upper floors.

The reflected light from one of those windows shows movement near the top of a tall elm. Straining to see Judith hears Lila's gasp as an echo of her own when a jean-clad leg disappears from the tree through an open window into a dark room. They have an anxious whispered conversation about the urgent need to stop Andy versus the wiser course of calling for help. After a few moments they agree that immediate intervention is required.

Neither of them has climbed a tree in years.

"I'll go up and you call 9-1-1 and knock on the door, telling them what's happened."

"No, I'll climb it I think I'm in better shape than you, I go to the gym."

"Stop wasting time, Lila!"

"I'm not letting you to go after him alone, Grant would kill me if anything happened to you."

"Oh he's already going to kill both of us for coming this far!" their nervousness makes them giggle at that remark. Judith jumps to grab hold of a low branch and swings herself up, already reaching for the next. The bark is rough under her hands and curiously wet. Sap? or something coming off of the crushed leaves? Lila is right behind and she can hear her saying she needs the police for an intruder and no, she doesn't know the address but can't they just trace her call?

The further up they climb the more difficult it becomes. Having just seen Andy scale the tree they know there is a way through but he's taller and has a longer reach. They struggle onwards and up, pausing to assess their route.

"What kind of tree is this anyhow?"

"It's an elm."

"Can't be, they all died out from Dutch Elm Disease."

"Not in Alberta, the province took measures to prevent that happening."

"Really? that was a−" but Lila is interrupt by Judith's hissed command to *keep quiet, we're here.*

They crouch together in a vee of branch and trunk, straining to see inside the dark room. There's enough ambient light to show that the screen has been pushed aside. They saw Andy come through here just moments before they arrived so they're also straining to hear any sounds from him.

Grabbing hold of a smaller branch above her head Judith lifts up her right leg and stretches it to the window sill and then over into the darkness. Her foot gropes for purchase finally touching a surface − a night table? no, too soft, a couch or a bed. With Lila steadying her hips she manages to get one hand on the window ledge and the other at the side, enough to swing her body in. She lands on a sofa and almost tumbles off but after a wobble keeps her balance. Turning back to the window she reaches out for Lila who has already got both legs on the ledge ready to slide into the room.

They've made some noise getting here so now they pause, breaths held, to listen. They hear stealthy movement in the next room. Then the connecting door is flung open and they're momentarily blinded by the bright fluorescent light of a bathroom but they can still see a tall silhouette.

"Stop!" yells Judith.

Just as Lila warns: "Police are coming!"

All the dark figure, Gary, hears are cries of *stop police* and he races out of the room. Judith and Lila are right behind him and Andy, having followed the women up the tree, has now jumped into the room in pursuit.

The hallway is dimly lit but Gary knows his way and goes thundering down the stairs. His pursuers have slowed slightly, none having ever been in the house before, and that hesitation means the subsequent injuries are less severe than they might easily have been. Gary has stopped on the landing and when the women close in on him he grabs and then pushes them out of his way. They fall right down that treacherously slippery staircase to the main floor.

The crashing of bodies and the high-pitched screams draws everyone into the great hall, including Grant and Reg who've just followed the 9-1-1 responders through the front door.

Standing just past the door Grant is stunned to see a tangled heap of bodies including Lila, moaning in pain, and Judith unresponsive and deathly pale. Gary, landing on his knees, now scrambles up and runs out the door. Andy chases after him. He freezes for a split-second when Moira's shriek of *Anton! no!* startles everyone, but then he's gone.

Reg and the two uniforms speed after the two men, one of them calling into his radio for an ambulance, and for back-up to capture suspects fleeing on foot.

Grant drops down beside Judith gently laying his hand on her throat, relieved to feel a pulse but afraid to move her. Beth painfully scoots backwards until she's propped up against the wall. There she relaxes some of the pressure on her upper body. When she meets Grant's eye she explains, through gritted teeth, that she's dislocated her shoulder. Sirens announce the arrival of several more police cars and the ambulance. That crew, a man and a woman, immediately demand everyone clear the area citing the authority of Covid-19 protocols.

Grant is ready to protest but a uniformed cop pulls him outside so the EMTs can do their job. The family members are finally dispersed from the hallway. After a few minutes of chaotic milling about the techs load both Judith and Lila onto stretchers and wheel them into the ambulance. There's no room for Grant despite him claiming to be Judith's fiance. Lila, already enjoying relief from the painkiller she's been given, smiles to herself thinking *I'll have to remember him saying that so I can tell Beth and Brian.*

Covid-19 Updates: All pensioned seniors will receive a non-taxable one-time payment of $300 to help offset added costs. 9 million in Federal funding goes to agencies providing delivery services for groceries, medications, toiletries, etc.. to seniors.

Chapter Twenty-Two

Wednesday, May 6, 2020

Anton Czerny, *aka Andy*, easily catches up with Gary Nichols but now that the police are involved instead of tackling the youth he runs right past him. Escaping lawful custody means he's guilty of an indictable offense and there is no statute of limitations on prosecuting that charge. So he continues to run, determined to get far away as quickly as he can.

Ever since Barbie's photo appeared in the news, a picture that included her family and specifically his girls, Anton has been surveilling the house. All the information included in the headline item made it easy for him to track them to their fancy new home in this rich suburb. He's been enjoying glimpses of his daughters, and keeps watching in the hopes that one or both will come into the back garden to give him a chance to meet them. It doesn't occur to him that the sudden appearance of a stranger in the privacy of their own yard would drive any female away screaming.

While lurking in the shrubbery he's seen the new husband, the stepson and the younger girls, Moira, and even heard Bonnie's voice on speaker during a call with Barbie which really surprised him. But on that fateful Tuesday he didn't see any stranger enter or leave, so he knew that Barbie's killer belonged in the house.

The police would like his testimony about those vital hours but Anton, successful in living on the run for more than a decade, continues to excel at evading capture. His daughters, having grown up in fear of their violent father, don't want a re-union. Neither of them are interested in finding out anything about the man who ran after Gary.

In the aftermath of the arrest Grant sits down with Moira to discuss the Anton Czerny situation. The Crown does not want him to *return to life* after an official declaration of death, and Moira decides that she really can't be certain it was Anton after all. Grant knows she is 100% certain it was him, but a dead man can't fight for custody and she only has a couple more years of having the girls at home. She isn't worried about their estranged father finding them back at home in Toronto.

Two police cars corner Gary who surrenders when faced with armed officers. Reg arrives as the handcuffed young man is bundled into the back of a cruiser. Sobbing that he didn't mean to kill her, but she made him so mad and he wasn't thinking straight or he'd have realized it was dumb thing to do. Reg advises Gary of his rights under the Canadian Charter.

"I want to talk to my Dad," insists the youth.

Reg points out that Gary is legally an adult but kindly adds that he'll let Greg Nichols know about the arrest and where they've taken his son.

Returning to the house he does notify Greg who appears utterly stunned by the news. Shawna, in the hallway jumping up and down with excitement, shrilly cries:

"Me and Sheila always knew it was Gary, I said so, too. We never liked him and we were right!" Her half-sisters shepherd the two younger girls upstairs, while Moira takes Greg by the arm and leads the shattered man to sit down.

Judith, still unconscious, is admitted to the hospital but Lila is treated in the back of the ambulance. Only emergency patients are allowed inside Alberta Health facilities. The paramedics did the job of wrenching her shoulder back in place and putting her arm in a sling to keep the painful area immobile, but need a doctor to sign off on the treatment.

During the twenty-minute wait in the parking lot Lila calls Brian to come pick her up. She'll worry about getting her car home tomorrow. Tonight she has to worry about Brian's angry disapproval of what she and Judith were up to, but hopes to play the injured victim card for some sympathy and tender loving care.

"You've been very lucky – again!" admonishes Grant. He's speaking gently because it's such a relief to hear Judith's voice. He has to be content with a phone call since no one's allowed inside the hospital. Tomorrow morning at 10:00 he'll be waiting in the parking lot after she's released.

Judith is suffering from a mild concussion but fortunately there is no swelling or brain damage, and no broken bones from the fall down the stairs. It turned out to be the same doctor who'd seen her back in March and the woman just shakes her head about Judith being accident-prone. No one bothers to correct her.

"Luckily I have a really hard head, I guess," answers Judith.

"Hard-headed as in stubborn? For sure! Oh, Judith," Grant pauses a moment and she can hear him take a deep breath. "It's pretty obvious that I'm going to have to take care of you from now on."

"Hmm, that sounds awfully bossy unless... Grant, is that a proposal?"

"No... but it's a promise."

Covid-19 Updates: City parks and children's playgrounds are closed off with yellow tape and can't re-open until they've had on-site safety inspections. Signage will be added promoting healthy best-practices.

The End

Don't miss out!

Visit the website below and you can sign up to receive emails whenever Della North publishes a new book. There's no charge and no obligation.

https://books2read.com/r/B-A-RNHX-YXXMC

BOOKS 2 READ

Connecting independent readers to independent writers.

Also by Della North

Village of Edgemont
A Deadly December in Edgemont
A Fatal February in Edgemont
A Sinister Spring in Edgemont

Watch for more at dellanorth.ca.

About the Author

Della enjoys mysteries that won't keep her up at night, have a hint of romance, and a satisfactory ending. Preferably in a series.

She and her partner live with a tuxedo cat in the sunniest city in Canada, nestled in the foothills of the Rocky Mountains.

In November of 2022 Della undertook the National Novel Writing challenge to complete a 50.000 word first draft and the Village of Edgemont series began.

Books in this series:

1 - "**A Deadly December in Edgemont**"

2 - "**A Fatal February in Edgemont**"

3 - "**A Sinister Spring in Edgemont**"

A portion of sale proceeds will be donated to NaNoWriMo.org in appreciation.

Read more at dellanorth.ca.